A Matter Of Form

William Babb

iUniverse, Inc.
New York   Bloomington

A Matter Of Form

iUniverse books may be ordered through booksellers or by contacting:

iUniverse
1663 Liberty Drive
Bloomington, IN 47403
www.iuniverse.com
1-800-Authors (1-800-288-4677)

ISBN: 978-1-4401-8411-6 (pbk)
ISBN: 978-1-4401-8412-3 (ebook)

Printed in the United States of America

iUniverse rev. date:11/9/09

CHAPTER ONE

The airport limousine swung into the double wide driveway of an expansive family home in west Waterloo. The driver alighted and opened the door to his only passenger, a tall dark haired young man, who gazed around him as if this was his first sight of the attractive place. From what he recalled of his home which now lay before him, he assessed that the front garden had been totally re-landscaped. As the driver handed his passenger the well packed carry-on bag he'd taken from the trunk, the door of the house opened and a middle-aged woman wearing a bright floral dress rushed out to hug the passenger.

"How lovely to see you, Simon!" she cried, her eyes bright and her smile wide.

"Hey, Mum! How're you? It's been such a long trip. I never thought I'd get here." The young man said rather breathlessly since his mother had squeezed him so tightly.

She stepped back and took his free hand. "Come on in, my dear. I'm sure you need a cuppa!"

Simon turned to find some change in his pockets and pay the driver before he was led into the house. He continued looking around as they entered the hall and then the kitchen.

"Gosh, Mum! You've made a lot of changes in the time I've been away. Aren't you ever satisfied with what you've got?"

She didn't answer but a secret smile formed on her lips as she turned to fill a kettle with water from the bright new faucet over the modern stainless steel sinks inserted in a polished granite counter top.

"You don't know how good it is to be back home, even if it has changed!" Simon said to her back. "I like what you've done to the kitchen."

"I'm really glad you're here, son. I've missed you terribly with nobody around much." She busied herself getting out the cups and saucers and pouring hot water into the tea pot.

"But you've got Dad and Sam. How come you missed me so much?"

She sat down at the kitchen table and served the tea. "You were here to talk to when you came in from school and, later, from university until you went away. But, even then, I saw a lot of you during vacation times. Dad's either at his office or at meetings with other health care people. Samantha's not much different. She works shifts at the hospital and in her spare time she's always out with one friend or another."

"I understand how that seems to make it lonely for you." Simon answered sympathetically. "But don't get your hopes too high for me as a shoulder to cry on! I've got to get launched in some career or other, you know!"

She blew across the top of her cup. "Golly, this tea's hot!" She put the cup into its saucer and leaned her elbows on the table to gaze closely at her son. He still had those piercing green eyes and curly brown hair she'd admired since babyhood.

"Of course, I realize that. Now you've finished all your university degrees, you're bound to want to get started on some rewarding work but don't rush at it, my dear. Take your time to look around. Study form, as it were!"

Simon sipped his tea. "This is the best cuppa I've had in a long time!" He smiled at his mother feeling affection in his heart while holding the cup in front of him. "I promise I'll take my time and be here for a good while yet to enjoy chats with you." Another sip. "But what did you mean about studying form?"

She laughed –a warm deep throated sound. "I was thinking of the fact that there's really a shape or arrangement or organization of things that makes up our way of life – y'know, there's some sort of form." She laughed again. "I don't know how else to explain it but you must have found many things different in England and need to re-adjust now you're home!"

"Mother! You're quite a thinker! You're also a worrier but I don't want you to worry over me." Simon stood up, walked behind her chair to put his hands on her shoulders. "Let me go to my room and get settled." He bent over to kiss her cheek. "When's Dad going to be home?"

"Oh, he should be in by six. I'll have dinner ready by then so don't stay upstairs too long, will you?"

Simon picked up his bag and left the kitchen without another word.

In the bedroom that he'd occupied since childhood he found nothing had changed. The drapes were the same as was the matching bed cover. Everything seemed to be exactly as he'd left it. Had his mother been keeping it as a shrine? he wondered as he reflected on the warmth of her welcome. He hoped not. True he loved his mother and she clearly loved him but he didn't want to become a man tied to her apron strings like several others he'd met while in London. They were always required to be present at home at weekends, while leaving him without a friend to go around with, in what was a completely strange and overwhelming city when he first encountered it on arrival from Waterloo.

He wandered around fingering the little awards and gifts he'd collected during his high school life. First he touched a certificate for editing the school journal for his final two grades which stated "*Awarded to Simon Lightward for dedication and excellence*". He had been very proud of that. Next he came to a cup for being in the winning team at football; then a tie-pin given to him by his date at the final school prom; and, finally, a large wall poster of the Toronto Blue Jays in their world cup year. Ah! Those were the days! He felt himself getting sentimental as his heart warmed to the memories. He wondered what did happen to that girl in high school after he left to go to Western University?

Now, after two years at the London School of Economics, he seemed to have lost all the connections he'd had. He located his old address book in the drawer of his dresser and thumbed through the names. For those he remembered well he speculated about what job they might be in, or whether they were married – even had kids, for God's sake! He'd been careless about keeping in touch while in University and in London but he might try to make contact with some now that he was back home, especially that girl from the prom – what was her name?

He kicked off his shoes and lay down on the bed. How good it felt after the hard lumpy one in his two-roomed furnished flat near the London School of Economics. Although he'd won a scholarship to pay his fees for the program in London, he'd had to rely on the generosity of his father for other expenses, and rents in London were atrocious when he had to convert the Canadian dollar to pounds. With the help of contacts he'd made in the college he was given a few hours of work a week helping in a store, where the owner paid him in cash so as to avoid completing an impressive array of Government forms to make him a regular part-time employee. Ah, yes! Those forms! He thought the British were even more prone to filling out forms than Canadians. What happened to the theory that computers would simplify the administrative procedures? Anyway, he'd survived with honour, he felt, and now at 25 he was a BSc (Econ) armed with enough education to run Research In Motion, given half a chance! He smiled at his thoughts but was realistic enough to know he must build some real life experience. He'd swam through the river of scholarship and must now jump into the ocean of employment.

There was a tap on the door and, before he could roll off his bed, it opened to allow his father to enter.

"Dad!" Simon exclaimed with delight, "You must be home early, otherwise we'd all be sitting down to dinner waiting for you!"

His Father, a tall, dark haired, heavily built man, grabbed his son around the shoulders and squeezed in a bear hug.

"Hey, m'boy! It's good to see you at last" He stood back to appraise his son. "My, you've put on some weight, I'll have to be careful!" He gave Simon a mock punch in his abdomen. "But don't be cheeky! I can still take you on in a bout or two of boxing or wrestling."

Simon remembered his Dad's favourite sports, even though he didn't practise them now. "I think it's all that English plum duff and

Yorkshire pudding they seem to give me with every meal!" He explained.

"Well, never mind that! Come downstairs. Mother's got a lovely piece of sirloin roast to celebrate the homecoming of our prodigal son!"

Simon put his arm around his Father's shoulders and together they entered the dining room where a table was set with a white linen cloth, silverware and crystal glasses. Mother came in and asked them to sit down.

"Will Samantha be joining us?" asked her husband.

"No. I'm afraid not, dear. She's on the middle shift at the hospital so she doesn't get off until seven. I'll save her a meal."

"Pity," commented her husband, "You'd think she could make an effort for Simon's first evening home. It'd be nice to have the family together at one time for a change."

When the carving dish of beef was put on the table in front of Father he took up a knife and cut generous slices for each plate. Then his Mother went round with dishes of roast potatoes and green vegetables to allow everyone to help themselves. Soon they were engaged in enjoying the delicious food and conversation languished.

After cleaning his plate, Simon remarked that he hadn't enjoyed food so much since he left home. "Somehow, I don't think the British people know how to cook," he said. "The beef's always too dry and the vegetables too soft!"

"Did you go out to restaurants to eat regularly?" asked his Mother as she gathered the empty plates.

"Not often, Mum. It was too expensive for me on my allowance. It was more likely to be McDonald's or Pizza Hut."

Father butted in. "I hope you're not implying my allowance to you was meagrely? My present financial state after seeing both you children through University is just about bare bones."

His wife laughed. "And if we stewed those down for soup we'd soon be in the poorhouse! Oh Mike, you do exaggerate!"

"HUH! Because I'm a doctor everybody thinks I'm wealthy. I have to provide an office, pay a receptionist and nurse out of the strict allowance the Government gives me to treat patients who look upon me as their personal slave!"

"Please don't complain, Mike. You do have me to manage your household with efficiency and economy! That's why we still pay our bills on time."

"Sounds to me as if you're getting a bit stale, Dad. Have you thought of retiring?" Asked Simon.

"WHAT ME? I'm only fifty-four y'know. What should we live on for the next twenty or twenty-five years?"

"There'd be pensions, surely? People like police, firemen, teachers and so on can retire at fifty-five. Why can't you?"

"Simon, you're still naive in spite of the LSE teaching. They get contributed pensions through their employers – namely us taxpayers. – I have to save for my own retirement."

Mother intervened. "Let's close this discussion, shall we, and go into the living room for a coffee?"

They at once pushed back from the table and went to find comfortable seats in the living room facing out through walkout doors to a serene garden while Simon's mother, Joan, prepared coffee. Before it was ready Samantha came in and marched straight up to her brother. Simon stood up and kissed his sister on the cheek.

"So how's my baby brother after all this time in wicked London? Did you have a good time with all the English girls? Are they really as cold as people make out?" she asked him scornfully.

"I'm none the better for seeing you!" he replied bitterly. "I had to work hard at my studies over there and didn't have time for a social life."

Then he added, "Haven't you landed one of those hospital doctors as your husband yet? I'd hoped to come back and find you gone."

His sister twirled to leave the room but turned back to face him again. "Let me tell you, brother, life is hard in the real world. You've been lucky to get an interesting two years in England while I've been on the wards with plenty of overtime. The government here keeps the hospitals short of money so they never have enough nursing staff and we can't give patients the kind of care they deserve. I certainly haven't had time to worry about a husband!"

Before she could leave, Mother came in with the coffee and said, "Are you two at one another's throats again? I'd hoped your absence would have made you want to end that, Simon."

"She's always belittled me and I won't put up with it. If she thinks I'm still a kid whose been spoilt by his parents, she's got to think again. My experience away in London certainly strengthened my self esteem and made me more independent."

His father blew his nose noisily and said, "Never mind that. What're you going to do with yourself now, Simon?"

"Frankly, Dad, I don't know. I've got to take the temperature of the water here and find out what's available by way of employment. I'm not sure what to reach out for – perhaps something to do with business or finance -- or I might be in computers. Give me some time, please! If you've got any ideas or contacts, I'd sure appreciate it, Dad."

"Sure. I understand you needing time to do some research but".. He waggled his finger under Simon's nose. "I want you to clearly understand, from the time you get a pay packet you're contributing to this household."

"Okay, Dad, I get the message. You're a tough nut to go against!"

CHAPTER TWO

Simon awoke to a showery summer morning. He peered through the rain-spotted window at the back yard which was mainly emerald green grass bordered by paving block paths or beds of shrubs. It all looked very fresh and inviting. 'I must take a walk' he thought as he slipped off his sleeping shorts and took a shower. After showering meticulously, he selected his newest grey pants which, he was pleased to find, still fitted him and a fresh plain t-shirt in green to wear for his outing.

Downstairs, in the kitchen, his father still sat over a cup of coffee reading the 'Globe and Mail'. He was wearing a white dress shirt and navy blue pants and looked up as his son entered. He was a handsome man with clear brown eyes beneath bushy eyebrows and a mop of dark hair tinged with grey at the side burns. "Did you have a good night, Simon?" he asked pleasantly.

Simon sat at the table before saying, "Yes, thanks, Dad. The bed was as comfortable as I remembered it."

"What would you like for breakfast, dear?" His mother asked brightly while straightening out her floral coloured apron. "I've got some nice ham that'd go well with eggs and hash browns."

"Hell, love, don't go spoiling him. He'll come to expect it!" His father commented with a laugh as he rose from the table and left the kitchen.

"Take no notice," instructed his Mother, "You enjoy what you want!"

"Then I'll have what you offered." said Simon.

His father had left the newspaper on the table so Simon grabbed it and quickly scanned the front pages. "Same old wars and worries," he declared disgustedly. "Don't papers print good news anymore?"

"Don't get to be a grouch, Simon. Take a positive outlook and find the cheerful news. It's there if you look for it," remarked his mother, looking over his shoulder while waiting for food in the frying pan to heat up. "There!" she pointed to a small paragraph headed '**Dog Saved From Pond**'. "That's good news!"

"Mother, you're a born optimist. I'll certainly try to follow your example!"

She served the breakfast and sat down with a coffee herself. Although in her fifties she still had a soft complexion devoid of all but the minutest creases alongside hazel eyes. "What are you going to do today, dear?"

Simon finished a delicious mouthful he was enjoying before answering. "I'm going to call one or two of my friends from university, if I can find them at home. I'd like to know what they've done and how they got jobs, if they're working."

"That paper you've got always has pages of 'Careers'. You might look through that first."

"Okay, Mum. I'll go into the living room and browse!" He finished clearing his plate, then stood up and grabbed for the paper as he gave his Mother a peck on the cheek before leaving the kitchen. "Thanks for an enjoyable breakfast, Mum!"

In the living room he chose an armchair with its back to the window and shook out the paper to the professional vacancies page. At first glance there did seem to be a wide choice of jobs but, after he had tired of reading 'qualified accountant' or 'appropriate experience' in every one of them, he threw it aside. He knew in his heart that his lack of experience at anything other than a coffee-shop jerk would be his shortcoming. He began to berate himself over not trying one of those casual opportunities that LSE had offered. They were usually short-term research assistants to professors or established companies in the City. They would have given him something relevant to put in his resume. Now, where could he start?

He went up to his room to find his address book and call Gerry Unger, an especially close friend at university. Would he be home or at work? Simon was delighted to hear him answer the phone. He pictured his friend as he had last seen him—short and chubby with a snub nose and wearing t-shirt and jeans. "Hello Gerry! How're you these days? Long time no see!"

"Is that you Spiffy?" came the squeaky voice. "Are you home from the promised land? We've got to get together and exchange news."

"That's why I'm calling, Gerry. Are you free for lunch today?"

"I seem to be free all the time! Having a hard time trying to get a job but I'd love a lunch! You're paying?"

"If we go to MacDonald's or Tim Horton's I can manage it. Shall we say the one on University Avenue?"

"The TH just east of Regina, you mean? All the U of W students seem to go there."

"That'll do fine! Say eleven-thirty?"

"Okay Spiffy! See ya' there"

Simon walked about five hundred meters to catch a bus and found Gerry waiting outside the Tim Horton's building, still in his usual garb of t-shirt and faded blue jeans. They exchanged warm hugs and Gerry pushed Simon towards the door. Inside it was being utilised by students and older couples and there was a short line-up to place an order. Simon asked for a sandwich and coffee for them both and paid. They took their meal to a vacant table.

Gerry stared at his friend and smiled. "My God, Spiffy! You've put on a few pounds since you've been away."

Simon laughed. "As I told my folks last night, it's all the Yorkshire pud 'nd potatoes!"

"I think you've had an easy time over there. I bet they don't work you like we were used to."

"It's true there aren't any physical activities in the LSE program and they don't play baseball, football or hockey, like any other civilized country, but they do like walking and soccer so I tried to team up with a group at weekends. What you're seeing is that I've matured!"

Gerry burst out laughing while trying to avoid spitting out the sandwich he was eating. "I don't know what maturing has to do with putting on weight. I think it's all the care your folks have taken over you in the past. You've always had the best they could do for you. Even now, you can still be smartly dressed and afford to pay for me. No wonder we all called you 'Spiffy'." He wiped his mouth with a napkin. "Even your sister always seemed to resent you."

Simon felt himself stiffen and become consciously guilty but he waved his hand across the table. "Forget all that, Gerry! What's been happening to you?"

"Me? I just can't seem to find work. My folks don't hassle me about it and they let me stay at home without giving any financial help but I've a feeling they worry about me." He took a drink of his coffee. "It's not that I haven't tried – I've been to the government employment office and checked out Workopolis on line—and I've applied for several positions but, alas, to no avail!"

"Is it that there aren't suitable jobs available or does your resume need fixing up?"

"OH, there's tons of jobs! You should go on line to the government web site. They list hundreds including plenty in the civil service."

"But you've not had a call to interview when you've applied?" pressed Simon.

"Not a sniff, old boy. I'm an unwanted species!"

"You mustn't get depressed," advised Simon as he screwed up his napkin and stuffed it into the coffee cup. "If you're ready, come with me right now. We'll go together to the employment office and check out what they have."

The two friends stood up and left the coffee shop. Outside Gerry said, "It's jolly good of you to want to help me but you haven't told me anything about your experience in England. When can we have a chat about that?"

"Not much to say, Gerry, but I expect I'll give you a briefing eventually! Right now my ulterior motive for helping you is to use your know-how to guide me around. My old man has issued an ultimatum that I must contribute to the household expenses once I get a job, so I don't think he'll be happy until I do!"

They caught a bus to the Government Employment Office which was some distance away in the downtown area and chatted and laughed together until they got there.

Once inside the building Gerry advised Simon to register. This involved completing a form which they got from a clerk at the counter and took to a table to work on. Most of it was personal details that presented no problem until it required Simon's social insurance number.

"What's this number they want?" Simon asked.

"Haven't you ever applied for one? Have you never been in a job where they needed your number to prepare your pay?"

"No, Gerry. I've only ever had casual jobs where I'd got paid in cash."

"And you've never had to file a Tax Return?"

"My God!" Simon exclaimed. "You mean to say that before I can earn an honest dollar I must be registered to pay tax on it?"

"Well, the SIN, as it's called, isn't all bad, it's needed when you want any benefits from the State. Eventually you'll need it to get an Ontario health card so you can get free medical care. Why don't you ask the clerk at the desk whether you can get the SIN here?"

"Well, if you say so. It's just one damned form after another!"

Simon got up and walked to the nearest available clerk where he asked about how to apply for a social insurance number. The clerk gave him the appropriate form and explained. "All the government services are integrated so we can process that application when you've completed it."

"Thank heaven for small mercies!" Simon mumbled as he walked back to join Gerry.

As soon as they started completing the form they met another snag. Simon pointed to a place on the form. "Look here, old fellow! They need my birth certificate or something to prove I'm really a Canadian but I've got nothing with me."

"I think you'd better take it home with you and we'll come back later." advised Gerry.

"Oh, hell! Nothing's simple, is it?"

"While we're here, let me show you all the job listings." Gerry stood up and waved a hand around the walls of the building. "See all those display panels? That's where you can read about different jobs and the companies offering them." He started to walk over to one wall and Simon slowly followed.

"Look at this one, Spiffy! Might suit you. It's in a Parks Department and requires operation of a power mower as well as edging round trees."

"What on earth does that mean?" asked Simon.

Gerry turned to face him, put his arms stiffly by his side and started a sideways shuffle in a circular motion. "I expect this is what they mean" he said to explain his humorous concept of the advert.

Simon laughed loudly and began to copy his movements. The other people were attracted by the noisy laughter and strange display. One tall and one chubby young man, slowly moving stiffly around in small circles, calling out to one another, " Here's another tree to edge round" and following it with another burst of laughter.

After a few moments, a manager came from his private office and told them to stop their antics. "If you two young men cannot behave responsibly, I'll have to ask you to leave."

"Sorry, sir," Gerry spoke up first. "It was my imagination ran wild when I read that advert." He pointed to it and the manager quickly scanned it. As he did so, a smile formed on his face and he walked away.

"Let's get out of here," Simon said abruptly. "I'd like to get off home and use Dad's computer to scan jobs on the various web sites. I think we might find something more suitable to our education."

"Well, if you say so, Spiffy. But don't get your hopes up!"

The two left the building and caught a bus to take them to their respective homes.

*　　*　　*　　*

Joan Lightward had spent a pleasant afternoon in the garden. She was an inveterate gardener and the modernization of the landscaping around the house was all her design. Although a contractor had done the work, she was always on his tail to keep things clean and tidy.

She had just completed the sweeping of paths after carefully mowing the grass areas when Simon strolled towards her.

"Hello, Mum. Did you enjoy your gardening today?" He gave her a peck on the cheek. "You didn't happen to edge round trees, did you?" He laughed, wondering whether his Mother would know what he meant.

She laughed too while answering him, "Like this?" and proceeded to gyrate in a similar manner to those the boys had used in the employment office. "Where did you see that phrase?"

"It was on an advert for a job in a Parks Department and Gerry thought it funny enough to demonstrate. I joined in but the manager didn't like us disturbing the office, so we left."

"Then you'll be ready for a cup of tea, as I am." She began to put her tools in a shed attached to the rear wall of the building. "Would you go and put the kettle on, son?"

"Okay, Mum. See you in the kitchen."

When she came in, she washed her hands and found the kettle boiling. She made tea and sat down at the table with her son. "So what did you do today?"

Simon told her all that had happened and asked, "Do you think Dad will let me use his computer to look up jobs on the internet?"

"I can't see why he wouldn't, especially as it's to look for a job!" She poured the tea for them. "So you found nothing in the Globe and Mail, then?"

No, Mum. They all need so much past experience. I've got to find something where I'll get training and experience."

"But doesn't your degree count for something?"

"If it was a professional designation, like accountant, it would get me something but my degree is only proof that I've got the stamina and intelligence to pass academic exams."

"Then, I don't see why you went the route you did?" His Mother observed.

"It's simply because I got that award that paid for my time at LSE."

"Hmm. If we'd have understood that, we might've persuaded you to take a professional course but I think we were swayed by the pride we felt when you got your award."

"Come on, Mum! Don't blame yourselves. In the long run my experience at LSE will be worth it to some company where my economics speciality will be valuable," Simon said with more confidence than he felt at that moment. "Besides I haven't seriously started looking yet!"

"Of course, dear. I understand. Now go and get ready for supper, so I can prepare it without interruption."

Simon stood and went upstairs into his father's office. The computer on the desk was obviously in a stand-by state so he decided to call up a web site for jobs that Gerry had mentioned to him. He felt sure his father would not mind. A few clicks of the keyboard brought to the screen the opening page of the government's job opportunities. It announced there were 14,169 available throughout Canada that day. He clicked to limit his search to Ontario and started to scroll through the items. He was surprised at how wide-ranging they were in the level of education and experience needs.

After about fifteen minutes of scrolling he stopped for a careful read of one that caught his interest. It was from a world-wide brokerage company that claimed to have received an accolade for one of the best 50 employers in Canada. They were looking for young people to become Financial Advisors and offered to send out a free CD explaining the opportunities. Simon felt that this was on the lines that he had in his mind. He liked financial and economic problems and enjoyed talking to people about their personal financial goals and plans. He immediately clicked onto their website and ordered a copy of the CD.

When he met up with his Father at supper, he said that he'd used the computer and requested this information CD.

"I don't mind you using my computer, Simon," his father declared, "as long as you don't try to get into my personal files. They are protected by a password, of course, so I doubt you'd have got to them." He stuffed a forkful of vegetables into his mouth before continuing. "You should have your own password to sign on to the computer and manage your own files. We must set it up."

Simon was just scraping the last morsel from his plate and said, "Rest assured, Dad, I wouldn't touch anything personal but it's a good idea for me to have access only to my stuff and the internet in general. That was a great help to search for jobs and I'm going to apply for one."

"I'm glad to know that but what is this company you're interested in?"

"It's McNeill and Sutherland. They're registered in Britain but operate internationally and have branches everywhere."

"Oh!" interrupted his mother while scooping out ice cream into dishes for their dessert, "Don't tell me you may be going away again!"

"They have so many branches, I'm sure I could start locally."

"I just hope you're right," she said as she placed the dessert in front of him.

"I'd like to see this CD when you get it, Simon," his father demanded.

"Okay, Dad. You'll be the first after me!" He finished his ice cream. "I'm going over to see Gerry this evening. See you later!"

"Okay, son," acknowledged his mother. "Don't be too late."

CHAPTER THREE

The day the mail delivered a package to Simon, he couldn't wait to see what was in it. He tore open the envelope and pulled out the contents. Anxious to get to the CD he skimmed the front of other documents and went into his father's study with the disc. He had already been assigned his own password to access the programs he needed, so he inserted the CD in a drive and the information it contained began to display automatically. The first page carried the company name of McNeill and Sutherland and was embellished by an artistic border with various statistics concerning their operations listed below. It was the next page that heightened Simon's attention because it explained the type of apprenticeship program that was offered. Next came an outline of company employment conditions and benefits that followed from the learning period and held out rewards that a successful advisor might achieve.

Simon sat back in the chair and considered all he'd read. He summed up the pluses and minuses and came to the conclusion that he'd like the work and the potential rewards. It was even possible that he could run his own business as a franchise rather than remain an employee.

He returned to the computer monitor and clicked on a symbol that indicated he wanted to apply. An application form was presented and he began the process of completing the answers to the questions. All went well until he had to supply his Social Insurance Number – the same problem he'd met at the Employment Office – so he dug out the form he had from them and, was about to complete it with the information he did not have on that occasion, when he caught sight of a web address he could use to apply. He closed off the CD while accessing the Government Web site. He found their opening page carried a number of links and he identified the one he needed. In a very few minutes he'd completed his application for a SIN number and was told it would be mailed to him in about a week. Whilst feeling encouraged by the Government's efficiency in accepting on-line applications he felt somewhat annoyed at the delay. He decided to complete the rest of his application to McNeill and Sutherland but leave the SIN blank. He thought it all so marvellous that he could do all this without filling out any paper forms.

When his Father came home and had eaten his supper, Simon told him what he'd done with the CD up to the point of applying for a position.

"You mean to say," his Father interrupted, "you can do all this without a signature on a form? How the hell do they know you're legitimate?

"Well, Dad, they do have my birth date and my e-mail address. I would have thought it nails things down pretty good!"

"That's all very well, Simon, but it seems to lack a formality and where will this record be kept? Do you think they'll print a copy for their files?"

Simon laughed. "I hardly think so! They'll have my application assigned a unique number and kept in the computer."

His father grew restless and stood up. "It all seems so informal to me! What if they interview you and want to keep a record , or they offer you a job with certain conditions attached. Where will all the information be stored?"

Simon grew surprised that his Father, a doctor with hundreds of patients, could not conceive of all records being kept on computer.

"Dad, the whole point of having an electronic information system is to be able to collect it in a logical way and save masses of files and forms. All of which take up space and cause lots of trees to be felled."

"I don't see how I could do that with my patients. I often make long notes detailing their symptoms and tests. How much space would that take on a computer?"

"Dad," Simon replied, "that computer you've got upstairs could hold all the pages of the bible and all the works of Shakespeare and have room left over."

"But I need to get to a particular patient to retrieve their story quickly. How could I do that?"

"Simple! Assign each person a unique number and save all documents related to them under that code."

"But, how will I know Missus Smith's code? There may be dozens of them!"

"Dad, there are untold number of ways to organise a coding system. You would have to sit down with an experienced person to explain your way of working so whatever they designed would be helpful to you."

His Father walked over to face his son. He looked him in the eye and said, "Could you set up something for my patients so I can stop cluttering my office with endless files and paper?"

Simon was stunned and took a step back. "Gee, it's good of you to ask, Dad, but I haven't actually done anything like that before. There are professional companies that will have already designed systems for Doctors like you. Why don't you talk to one of them? It shouldn't be too costly."

"Hmm!" The Doctor rubbed his chin, "If I hired somebody, would you sit in and monitor what they might recommend?"

"Of course I would! I'd be honoured to help after all the help you've given me, Dad." Simon smiled and continued, "Of course, if I get a job, my time may be limited! Would that be okay?"

"Oh, sure, son. We'd work something out together." He clapped his son an the shoulder. "You go ahead with this thing you're interested in and I'll find out about these specialists that can help."

"Thanks, Dad." He turned to leave. "I'm afraid I must go out now. I'm meeting some old university pals at the local pub."

Simon headed off to the appointment he'd arranged through Gerry Unger and looked forward to the evening of camaraderie with friends he hadn't seen for two years.

*   *   *   *

The pub they had chosen to meet at was the "Fish and Fiddle" in downtown Waterloo. Gerry had said that this evening there was a special on chicken wings and Simon found his mouth watering with the thought of a glass of ale to wash down a plate of spicy wings. He took the bus from near his home and entered to find four familiar faces sitting at one table with an empty chair ready for him. The three whom he hadn't seen since his return stood up and there was a noisy scuffle of back slapping and joshing between them. It was not until a waitress appeared that they all took their seats and placed an order.

There was a period of casual and insignificant chatter, mostly directed to guesses about Simon's time in London, before their glasses of beer were put in front of them. After all raised their glasses and toasted the return of Simon the Spiff to the gang, Gerry suggested that they each took a turn to say what they were now doing. He concluded with, "Well I'll go first because I've not done a thing, so my turn is soon over!"

"You lazy bugger!" Shouted Roy Helwig, the tallest of the group, "No wonder you're so fat and round! If you worked hard like me, you'd be tall and lean!"

Gerry responded, "It wasn't for want of trying – you ask Simon!"

At that moment Simon was in close conversation with Terry Wong who was sitting next to him, so no one jumped to Gerry's aid and Roy teased him further by saying, "I'd say it was you was trying – trying to dodge work!"

"That's very unkind of you, Roy," Vernon Spreitzer spoke up in Gerry's defence. "I expect you only got a job because you were tall enough to change lamps in street lights without a ladder!"

Roy reacted. "And you, Vernon, are only waiting for God to make a big deposit in a Swiss bank before you find something!"

Simon heard the last remark and said, "I'm going to get a job as financial advisor with a big brokerage firm, so you guys have got to earn big money so's I can tell you what to do with it."

"Huh! I wouldn't trust Simon with my money!" shouted Vernon, "He's never known what it's like to save, coming from a rich doctor father!"

"Hey, you guys," Terry intervened. "Stop all this back-biting and let's eat our wings! The waitress is coming now."

They all sat back while the waitress set out serving plates of hot wings and individual side plates for each of them. Hands flashed out to grab a favourite flavour and the men were quiet for a while.

"Which of us has a good job with career prospects?" asked Terry at last. "Do you know what Confucius says? 'Choose a job you love and you will never have to work a day in your life' – any of you found that yet?"

"Yes, I have," answered Roy. "I'm an apprentice architect and every day is so exciting. I'll be fully qualified in two more years."

"That sounds wonderful," said Simon. "I hope my choice will be as good as Roy's"

"Vernon, you're quiet now. What're you doing for a living?" asked Gerry.

"Well, although I got my B.A., I fancied something practical. So now I'm an apprentice heating and cooling engineer. I like the changes the different assignments make to the problems you have to solve." He broke out into a wide smile before continuing. "Best of all, I've got married!"

There was a chorus of congratulations and comments on the opinion of some of his friends about the wisdom of such a state.

"And you, Terry?" asked Simon at last.

"My Father is a naturalist doctor and I'm studying how everything in nature can be used for healing our bodies. I have many courses to take but, right now, I help in making up medicines. This is only mechanical – just putting prescribed herbs or liquids into jars or packets – but eventually I too will become a naturopath."

Gerry stood up. "Gee, you guys have all found something interesting. I really wish I could get started."

Simon said, "Let's raise our glasses to wish Gerry good luck in finding a job soon. I feel so sorry that he's still at loose ends. And let's all wish Vernon a very happy life in the job of his choice and with a lovely wife." At this point he stood with the rest and added, "Let's all promise to meet here again in a month's time and have some fun."

They all raised their glasses and wished Gerry and Vernon the best of luck.

CHAPTER FOUR

Fifteen days after the group had gathered for a re-union, Simon received an e-mail from McNeil and Sutherland inviting him to an interview at the Holiday Inn in Kitchener.

He e-mailed acceptance and prepared for the day by studying the financial pages of the 'Globe and Mail.' His idea was to have a grasp of the current economic situation so that he could sound knowledgeable if asked questions. His LSE education gave him an overall view of macro-world economics but he hoped to relate that knowledge to more local matters.

On the day of the interview he dressed in a smart suit, shirt and tie that he assumed was the appropriate dress for business people in finance. He took a bus to the hotel and entered with some fluttering of his pulse. This would be his big test and he silently prayed he'd be accepted. The notice board in the front lobby gave the number of a room which had been reserved for McNeil and Sutherland, so he made his way there, with the guidance of various signs in the corridors, and respectfully knocked on the door. He waited for a few moments thinking the room may be empty and knocked again. The door was opened by an attractive young woman dressed in a floral print frock just reaching to the top of her knees. He was surprised to see such informality of business dress and stepped back slightly.

"You must be Simon Lightward," she said with a warm voice and a smile. "Do come in!" She stood aside to let Simon enter.

The room was no larger than a typical hotel room but furnished with one desk and two chairs. A man who was sitting behind the desk wore an open-necked shirt and stood up to meet Simon. "I'm Henry Allbine," he said, offering Simon his hand, "and this is my personal assistant Penny Fairweather. Come and take a seat."

Somehow Simon had pictured the interview to involve several senior-looking men, smartly dressed and sitting behind a desk with the applicant sitting in front of them. Here, there was only one other chair available which had already been placed alongside the one Henry had relinquished. He hesitated to occupy it, since he assumed it was being used by the woman assistant but she made it clear to him that he was to sit there by saying, "I'm going to rustle up some lunch while you guys have a chat!" and leaving the room.

"Come here Simon. We can use the desk together if we need to write anything."

Simon sat, feeling somewhat bewildered by the informality and thought this must be a preliminary step in considering him for training. Then he noticed a computer on the desk with a web-cam mounted on top. Was his interview being recorded? he wondered.

Henry had settled in his chair and began to explain things to Simon. "You may think all this is unusual, Simon, but we shall chat together in front of this computer and we shall be seen and heard by two of the company's senior managers in London, England. Do you have any objection to that?"

"Err, No! I'm surprised by the method you use but encouraged to find you so forward-thinking. Is this my one and only interview?"

"Certainly! You're only being considered for a trainee, so it's a test to see whether you are smart, coherent, articulate and intelligent. Your real test for permanent acceptance by the company will be your performance over your training period."

"I understand what you've told me. Can I ask your position in the company?"

"Sure," replied Henry. "You can ask any questions you like! I'm a local financial advisor here in the Waterloo Region."

"So you're a front line manager in the company – the kind of person I might be attached to for training?"

"That's exactly right, Simon. You assess situations pretty fast, don't you?" He gave Simon an encouraging smile. "Now, you've kind've taken control of our interview, so I'd like to ask you questions if you don't mind!"

Simon quickly recognised that Henry had a good sense of humour in the way he made these comments, so he relaxed a bit and smiled back as he said, "Go ahead!"

For the next twenty minutes, or so, they exchanged information in a friendly fashion, both personal and financial, none of which embarrassed Simon until he was asked, "Why didn't you give us your SIN on your application?"

"Ohh! I hadn't got one at that moment. I'd just applied to the government through their web site - but I have it now."

"I see," said Henry. "Can I see it please?" Simon found the card and passed it over. Nothing more was said and Jenny arrived with boxes of lunch and drinks. She also had a bell-boy in tow that put another chair in the room. This enabled all three to share a convivial lunch. They chatted about the weather and baseball, the Toronto Stock Exchange and the rising value of the Canadian dollar. The whole time Simon felt quite comfortable and added his share of comments on every subject.

When the meal was over and Penny began collecting the garbage, Henry said, "Penny is my assistant at present but she has completed training and been appointed to another office. How do you feel, Simon, at becoming my assistant to replace her?"

Simon almost fell off his chair with surprise which Penny noticed and said immediately "Don't rush to answer, Simon. You should hear what I think of him as a boss!"

"Henry intervened. "No you don't, Simon. She's much too prejudiced. You have to make your decision on our discussions this morning. After all, I was as much being tested as you were!"

There was a long moment of silence before Simon spoke up. "Would I have to do those jobs that Penny has done today?" Inwardly he considered them rather menial and not his idea of a financial advisor trainee.

"Yes you would and many other mundane jobs as well but you'll learn a lot through your interaction with other people. Understanding people is what it's all about!"

Simon remained pensive for a moment longer before he said, "Considering all the risks involved, I would like to accept the position as your assistant, providing it is for my training and ultimate appointment as a financial advisor."

"That's understood! Now, go out with Penny while I await the response of my Managers on this computer."

The two left the room and Penny said, "You're doing a smart thing to join this company. They're the best in the world!"

Shortly after, Henry opened the door and joined them. "I've got the okay to hire you, Simon. Can you start the first of the next month?"

"Can I just!" exclaimed Simon. "I appreciate your confidence in me and shan't let you down!"

"You'd better not, young fella! See you on the first." They shook hands and Simon walked on air as he left the room.

He did not notice the bell-boy advancing smartly along the corridor carrying on his shoulder a large tray of dishes. They collided just beyond the door of the room and there was an immediate dispersement of the tray's contents over a wide area of the carpet, followed by a loud clanging as the tray itself ricocheted from wall to wall and head to head until it reluctantly settled over a group of cups. The two young men had impacted with such a force that they were both stunned and were slow to realize their predicament. Penny poked her head cautiously around the door frame to ascertain the reason for the noise that she and Henry had heard and exclaimed, "What on earth happened to you two guys?"

Simon struggled to his feet and said, rather lamely, "It's my fault! I left you in a daze and ploughed straight into this fellow here." He shook his head. "I'm so sorry!"

"Don't worry," shouted Penny, "I'll call housekeeping."

The bell-boy stood up cautiously and surveyed the disaster of smashed or cracked dishes. He was glad they were clean ones. He could just imagine the scene if they had remnants of food on them to spatter the walls and carpet. He turned to Simon. "Look. I'm real sorry I didn't see you. Holding that big tray with my arm raised, I couldn't see much."

Henry came out of the room and picked his way cautiously through the carnage. "I don't think it's anyone's fault, really. You get off home, Simon, and I'll see that this is all cleared up by the hotel people."

Simon took a few steps away from him and looked back. "Thanks very much! I feel I haven't made an impressive start!"

"Off you go!" called Henry. "And watch where you walk when you get outside! I'd like to know you'll be intact when you come to work for me!"

*   *   *   *

Simon arrived home safely and gave his mother a brief sketch of his interview. She hugged him when he said he'd got the job. His sister, Samantha, entered the kitchen and asked, "What's all the fuss about, Mum. I wish I could get big hugs like that!"

"Oh, Sam! Don't be like that! I've hugged you many times in the past but this was special for Simon. He's just landed his first job."

"Sorry about that! – You know how quick I am to take umbrage?" She moved over to Simon. "Hey, Bro! Let's give you a hug and congrats on your first job!" Simon was surprised by her approach as he'd learned to be defensive of her in their younger days but he closed his arms around her and felt a genuine response in her hug. They moved apart and she said, "What've you landed and when do you start?"

"Come into the living room and I'll tell you," Simon said while walking out the kitchen door. Samantha followed and sat in an armchair opposite him. "This is quite a unique experience, Sam. All too often we would walk away from one another in a huff!"

"I know, Simon! I've been on courses at the hospital to help me amend my bitchy nature. It seems I was getting under the skin of my fellow workers and some doctors!"

"I'm so glad to hear that, Sam. You're a lovely woman and it would be awful if your personality ruined your future. Who talked you into the psych. program?"

His sister drew back in her chair with a frown on her face. "I think the biggest influence was a doctor I was dating. I really thought we were going to be together for ever but he corrected me over something I did on the ward and I flew off the handle. Then we stopped dating and I wanted to get him back so fervently that I joined this remedial psychology course. You've already noticed a difference in me, I'm sure!"

"Sis! I can't tell you how delighted I feel to find you so changed. May you go on benefiting from the course in the future." Simon stood up and gave his sister an affectionate peck on the cheek. "I love you, y'know!" He resettled himself in his chair. "But let me tell you about my job!"

"Thank you, Bro! I love you too! Now tell your story!"

He explained everything to her from seeing the advert to the interview but omitted his collision with the bell-boy. "I took to the guy who did the interview and who I will work with. I start the first of the next month," he concluded.

"It sounds like a great opportunity," Samantha observed, "and all this was done through a computer! You didn't have to complete or sign any forms?"

Their father came into the room and heard the last comment. "Mother's told me you've got a job, Simon. Congratulations, son! But what's this about not signing any forms?"

"Well, thanks, Dad! Everything's recorded on the company's computer. My whole interview, my personal information and my acceptance of the position."

Doctor Lightward shook his head in dismay. "Sorry, son, but I don't trust the setup. You might turn up for work and be told they've changed their mind. You've no security. It's a very fishy business!"

"Well, I don't know, Dad. When I was taken on as a nurse I didn't sign any papers except to enrol in the union or for extended health insurance." Samantha intervened to support her brother.

"Let me ask you something, Dad," said Simon. "Do you make new patients sign anything when they come to see you for the first time?"

His father thought a moment before answering. "NO! I don't do I! A file is opened for them and personal details recorded but I don't undertake to see them whenever they come in. It's a matter of trust!"

"Well, isn't that the same in my case?" Simon challenged him.

"But there's no paper record for you."

"The record is in the computer and there it will remain until it's expunged." Simon stood up and felt he'd scored a point, so he added, "You could keep all your patients' information on computer and save having all those folders taking up umpteen square feet of space in your office, apart from the need to cut down hundreds more trees!"

"I wish they'd do that in the hospital I work in. There are so many forms and folders that we're constantly having to make more space in the nurses station to hold them. I can just imagine how convenient it'd be to bring up the patient information on a computer monitor. No more mis-sorted or mislaid folders!"

"Samantha, my girl," her Father responded in his best authoritative voice, "It wouldn't work! Who's going to input all this information from several different sources to keep the files up-to-date?"

"It could be co-ordinated, Dad. A complete system would have to be designed but that's not beyond the powers of man, is it? Think of the complicated systems needed to bring about the space program. Every problem has been resolved to achieve an international space station."

"Think of the cost, too! We'd never get enough money to build an integrated medical system. We're always short of something!"

Joan Lightward quietly entered the room and picked up on the last comment. "Yes, and I'm short of help in the kitchen! Who'll peel the potatoes?"

This made them all laugh and Samantha left with her mother as a silent volunteer.

CHAPTER FIVE

The following day Simon went to see Gerry at his home. He found him guiding an electric lawn mower over the front grass of the home. "What's got into you, Gerry! You're working!" he chided as he walked up the drive. In his good natured way he switched off the power to the mower and hurried to give his friend a hug. "Although you're rude to me, I'm glad you came."

"Well, I've had my job interview and I've wondered if you've found anything?" Simon glanced at the idle lawn mower. "Except for that thing, of course!"

Gerry's usual smiling face collapsed into a hang-dog attitude. "Sorry, Simon! Nothing yet!"

"Come and have a coffee and tell me what you've tried."

The friends put arms around one another's shoulders and walked to the nearest Tim Horton's in the corner plaza of a main street. Once inside and sitting at a table with their coffees, Simon couldn't wait to tell his news. "I got hired yesterday! First interview! Can you believe it?"

Gerry finished his first sip of the hot drink and smiled. "I've always said you're the luckiest guy alive! If you fell down a sewer you'd come up with a Mars Bar!"

Simon laughed, took a sip, and said, "But tell me your troubles, old friend. I wish I could help."

Gerry sat back in his chair. "After our group meeting in the Pub the other week, I've been ashamed of myself and couldn't help think about the jobs those other guys had got. There's Roy going into architecture, Vernon's messing with heating and cooling engineering, and Terry is following in his father's footsteps to become a naturopath doctor." He closed his eyes and shook his head. "I've applied for several jobs but never got interviewed. What am I to do, Simon?"

Seeing Gerry's face and hopeless demeanour, Simon felt moved with the strong desire to help him get something. He felt afraid that his friend would sink into a depression. He spoke confidently. "Look here, Gerry, we can't have you in this state of mind. Until I have to start my job, I'm going to work with you every day to get you placed somewhere. So, cheer up, old lad. We'll finish our coffee and make a start on getting you a job!"

The Holiday Inn was within reasonable walking distance and Simon started out to go there first. On the way he recounted the story of how he'd made a complete ass of himself when he crashed into a bell-boy carrying a tray of dishes. The pair were laughing with intermittent guffaws as they sauntered along and embellished the story with their own imagination. In a gap in the cross-talk Gerry suddenly asked, "Where are you taking me, Simon?"

"We're going to the Holiday Inn to ask about vacancies on their staff."

"You think I might get the job of cleaning up all those crocks you broke?"

Simon was glad Gerry seemed to be taking the idea with a sense of humour. "No. I think they're long past recovery! I just want to find out whether there are vacancies, what jobs they are, and how we go about getting you one of them."

"That's all very well, my friend," said Gerry as he stopped suddenly, "but supposing I don't like the work? And, if I do, how will you set about trying to secure one for me?"

"Gerry, I'm flying by the seat of my pants! I can't answer your questions. Just go along with me and we'll see what happens, okay?"

Gerry nodded and they resumed walking. Ten minutes later they entered the lobby of the Hotel. Simon walked straight up to the reception desk which was not busy at that time of day and asked loudly, "Could I see the personnel manager please?"

A man dressed in shirt, tie and pin-striped blue suit standing behind one end of the counter looked up and addressed Simon. "Why do you want to see the personnel manager, sir?"

"I would like to know if you have any vacancies on the staff here."

The man moved along the desk to be opposite Simon. "You're taking a very unusual approach, sir. Most of our recruiting for managerial positions is done nationally. I can give you an address to write to."

"Thank you for the compliment you pay me by assuming I'm looking for a managerial position but, what I really need for my friend over there is something more immediate."

The man lifted his eyes to look at Gerry who stood a few feet back, attired in his traditional blue jeans and tee-shirt. "Is he not capable of seeking his own job?" He asked with a hint of superiority in his voice.

"Oh, yes. He's quite capable of speaking for himself. He is a graduate of Waterloo University but is having great difficulty in finding work." Simon looked back at Gerry and beckoned him over. "If you will tell him what jobs are available here, Gerry will tell you which one he'll take!" Simon knew he was being very audacious but hoped that the polite manner of his conversation might gain serious attention.

The man studied Gerry and asked, "What did you major in?"

"Maths and economics." Gerry answered calmly.

The man sifted through a few papers out of sight below the reception desk. "If you would consider becoming a night auditor on the desk here, I might be able to use you. Can you come back at ten this evening, preferably without your side-kick and decently dressed?"

Simon was tempted to intervene but remained tight lipped as Gerry answered "Certainly, sir. I'll do all I can to help!"

Next morning Simon was aroused from a deep sleep by his Father shaking him. He raised himself up out of his stupor and asked, "What's happened, Dad? House on fire?"

"No Simon , it's one of your blasted friends wants to talk to you. I wish you'd get your own cell phone!" He marched out of the room and slammed the door of the parents' bedroom effectively making sure his wife was aroused as well.

Simon had to go down to the kitchen to answer the phone and on the way he speculated it might be Gerry. "Hope he's not bringing me more trouble." he said to himself as he snatched up the handset. "Simon, here! Do you know what time it is?"

"It's Gerry." Came the bright and cheerful voice. "I know it's only just after seven o'clock but I couldn't wait to tell you I worked at the hotel last night and the guy you spoke with is taking me on a month's trial."

Simon felt extremely relieved. He knew he'd taken a big chance yesterday when he took Gerry into the hotel and spoke for him but, if you don't try something unusual, you never know what can be achieved. "I'm so pleased for you, Gerry. Did you like the work you did last night?"

"Oh, sure! Apart from feeling damned sleepy now, it was not hard and quite interesting. That fellow you spoke to is the manager here. He seems like a nice guy. He pointed out that we didn't follow form by applying for a job the way we did and said not many people would have listened to us."

"Then I guess, for once, we struck it lucky! There're too many forms to follow in this world, anyway! Tell me all about it when we have the next gang meeting."

"Sure thing! I'm off to bed now. Thanks a lot, Simon!"

Simon replaced his handset, looked at the time, and decided he might as well take a shower and get dressed. He thought he'd ask his sister about a cell phone, of which he was completely ignorant, and talk to his Dad about a car.

The opportunity to do both those things arrived at breakfast. He was sitting at the table eating cereal when Samantha came in. "Hey, sis. You've got a cell phone, haven't you? Tell me about it!"

Samantha was ready for her morning shift at the hospital and pulled her cell phone out of the pocket of her uniform. She pushed it over to her brother and said, "Here you go! Have a look at it!"

Simon twisted it around in his hand looking for a way to open the thing. Suddenly he found a small recess and flipped it open. It displayed the phone carrier's emblem. "So how do I make a call?" he asked.

"Punch in the number and press the phone button, you blockhead!" She went on to explain the principles and some convenient features and said, "It'll cost you money each month, y'know!"

"Well, I'll soon be getting a pay cheque, so I can afford it!" He passed the phone back to his sister. His father had come in so he said to him, "I've just been asking Sam about cell phones. I'll get one as you suggested!"

"Thank God!" Michael Lightward said grumpily. "Maybe I won't be woken up too early again!"

'Strike while the iron is hot' thought Simon. "Dad, do you think you could help me buy a car?"

The Doctor slammed his knife and fork down on the table with such force that it shook everything. "NO, I CAN'T!" he bellowed. "I've supported you long enough. If you need a car go and lease one!"

Somehow, Simon realized he'd chosen a bad moment and he excused himself and went up to his room. He pulled out his one bank account statement and cheque book and vowed to spend the day resolving those two problems. During his time at LSE his father topped up the account as it became necessary but, since his return home, nothing had been added. The balance now stood at $483.90. After his quick search of a shopping mall offering several booths selling cell phones, he walked to the nearest one and approached an assistant to buy a cell phone. Eventually, the moment came in the transaction when it was time for payment.

"Are you going to charge this to your credit card, sir?" asked the assistant who was a charming and attractive young lady. Simon gazed at her while he tried to find something to say. "Is that a problem, or are you just stricken by my beauty?" she added.

"Err, no! - - I mean, yes I am stricken by your beauty, and yes, there is a problem!" Prior to his having decided to buy the phone, he hadn't considered the mode of payment and this transaction not only required the initial purchase of the item but a recurring monthly fee which was to be charged to his credit card. "You see, I have a bank account but no credit card. Could I not have it all charged to my bank?"

The assistant became very business-like. "That's difficult to arrange because we would have to have a specimen of your cancelled cheque to make sure the monthly charges were debited to the correct account." She gazed at him with wide round eyes. "Do you understand?"

Simon understood but hadn't got his cheque book with him. "I hear what you're telling me but I think we must cancel the deal as I haven't brought my cheque book with me."

"Oh! I'm sorry about that. I hope you'll come back when you're more prepared!" She turned away and he caught her whisper to another assistant, "He looked all right but turned out to be a nerd!"

In spite of this set-back, Simon decided to go to a car dealership and find out their needs. He had seen adverts on television for cars needing "No Deposit" or "No Cash Down" so he wanted to explore. He chose a Ford dealership as his father always chose that make of car when he bought a new one. He strolled around the outside display and admired the shiny, gleaming, beckoning prospects. He was conscious of the need to have something economical since his initial earnings would be modest, so he studied a 'Focus' which was green and attempted to open the door to sit inside.

"Excuse me, sir!" said a salesperson who had been watching his peripatetic meanderings for some time, "We have all our outside cars locked up. Please come into the showroom and I can let you examine a 'Focus' there. They come in a range of colours and options, so you'll get just what you want" She extended a hand to him. "My name is Sally Field and I'm here every day."

Simon shook the proffered hand and studied the woman more closely. She looked about thirty with blond hair and blue eyes, dressed in a cool linen suit of palest blue. "Pleased to meet you. My name is Simon Lightward."

"I think I know that name. We have another customer of the same name. I think he's a local Doctor. Do you know him?"

"I suspect he's my father but don't mention I've been here if you see him. He made it clear he wouldn't help me to buy a car this morning!"

"Not to worry, sir! You could always lease one if you can't afford a purchase. It's quite the normal thing for people to do that these days."

They entered the showroom and Sally opened the door to a 'Focus' for Simon to sit inside. He did this and found it most comfortable and the dash conveniently laid out. He turned around and checked the back seats and asked a few relevant questions based on what his friends had mentioned about their cars. Finally he got out and Sally conducted him to her desk.

"I think you're very interested in that car, Simon. Would you like to take it for a test drive?"

Simon felt as if the floor had opened and he'd dropped about fifty feet. The question of actually driving had never entered his head. "B-But I don't drive! Couldn't you run me around a bit to get the feel of it?"

Sally smiled at him and shook her head. "I could do what you ask but how will you be able to use the vehicle if you can't drive?"

"When I've got it I can learn. It seems to make sense to me to learn on the vehicle I'm going to drive!"

"I wouldn't recommend that. Learners can often damage a vehicle when learning. You wouldn't be too happy to damage that nice new car, would you?" She was peering at him in a motherly way, as if to understand his naivety. "Tell you what. I run a driving school when I'm not needed at the dealership. Why don't you let me give you a few lessons to get you started?"

Simon was surprised but recognized the good sense of it. "Thank you very much! I'd like to take you up on that. Will it cost me much money?"

"I would suggest a dinner for the two of us after each lesson! How's that?" She spoke saucily and was grinning broadly.

"It's a deal! When can we start?" Simon replied with alacrity.

"Here's my card. Give me a call tomorrow and I'll set a date."

CHAPTER SIX

It was the first of the month and Simon's first work day. He took a bus to a small shopping plaza in Kitchener and scanned the shop names for McNeill & Sutherland. Towards one end of the row he spotted the banner name over a double-fronted unit and made his way towards the door set mid-way between the pair of windows. He thought it far larger than he had expected so was careful to inspect the name engraved on the glass panel of the door. Sure enough it said "Henry Allbine, Financial Advisor" so he entered.

To his left was a fairly spacious office with walnut furniture, the main part of which was a receptionist desk carrying a computer terminal. Behind this was a credenza unit covered by printers, fax machines and another device he couldn't identify, with file drawers beneath the whole thing. He turned around to look in the opposite room and found it almost identical but with fewer machines. Set deeper in the building was a conference room and a small kitchen. He spun round when the door opened and was surprised to see Penny standing there.

"Well, Hi!" he said. "I didn't expect to see you here!"

"Henry thought I should spend the morning guiding you through the common activities while you were getting accustomed to the work." She flung off her outer coat and hung it on a stand in the corner.

"That's jolly decent of him to do that. What about your own new position?"

She laughed. "I've rented a space in a new mall for my office and it won't be ready for another month. Right now I'm working out of home. When I explain some things to you you'll realize that my situation is very inconvenient."

"Oh, I see." said Simon, although he didn't understand the implications of her situation at all. "Shall I pull up this chair to sit beside you at the desk?"

Penny had already occupied the chair behind the desk and shifted across to let Simon do as he suggested. Once settled she turned on the computer. "Now, all the local offices are serviced by a master computer in London, England, but each operative must sign on with his own name and password. Since you are not logged in yet, I'll use my name and code to open the page where you can get set up."

Simon watched her do this but understood neither of her sign-on words that she entered before the page she called up, for a user to establish his log-in name and password, appeared on the screen.

"Why don't you choose what you're going to use and enter it into that form. If there's no conflict with anyone else, it will shut down to allow you to open under your signature, as it were."

Simon complied and in a matter of a few seconds the monitor blacked out and then returned with the log-on page. He entered his chosen codes and the home page opened before him.

"From here," explained Penny, "you can go to any area of service the head office provides, which includes accessing all of Henry's client information. I cannot emphasize too strongly that you're in a position of trust and must never reveal what you learn."

Henry Allbine, himself walked in and caught her last few words. "Thank you, Penny. You've said the most important thing. I hope you'll take this very seriously, Simon. I'll repeat it until you're bored as we work together!" He threw his jacket into his office and added, "How about a coffee?"

Penny laughed and stood up. "This is one of the most important aspects of your job, Simon! Making tea or coffee when Henry needs it or has a conference."

Simon stood up and squeezed behind their chairs to go into the kitchen. Penny followed and explained just what he should do. Since he had catered for himself in England, he figured he'd know everything he should but Penny soon disabused him of that idea and described exactly how coffee should be made.

After a few more words of general guidance and further instruction concluded, Penny left to leave Simon reading information bulletins on the monitor or some that came through by fax. The latter he passed to Henry immediately since they always seemed to refer to stock or bond issues. His only reaction to all this information was that he would need to be a millionaire to ever become an investor. Where did all the money come from? He asked himself.

After lunch, Henry had his first client. He was an elderly gentleman with thinning grey hair and a problem with his posture. Simon opened Henry's door and told the client to go right in. Henry looked up form his desk and expressed alarm. "Simon I'd rather you didn't just show my clients directly in to me when they arrive, I was in the middle of a tricky negotiation on the phone, just then."

Simon blushed and retreated. His first blooper of the day! After that client had gone, Henry admonished Simon again but said he was forgiven as it was his first day. He did, however, say that he would have expected Simon to have known the proper form in which to handle clients coming to visit him as a matter of common courtesy.

Around four o'clock, Henry came to join Simon at the reception desk. "In a few days, Simon, you will receive in the mail an American Express credit card in your name."

"Wow!" interrupted Simon. "That's just what I needed!"

"Just let me explain, before you get wild ideas. This card is issued to all employees and the size of the credit limit varies with their status. I think you'll be set at $2,000. This is intended to cover your business expenses, such as travel or meals. If you use it for personal items you'll receive a bill from head office to repay personal costs."

"How will they know what expenses are personal?" asked Simon. "Say I wanted a cell phone and charged it to my card, would they bill me later for re-imbursement?" He had in mind his recent embarrassment when shopping for a phone.

"The truth is, Simon, that they can't really tell what charges are business and what are personal. If the head office guy spots something unusual, he'll phone me and check it out. Anything that remains paid for by the company is eventually debited to my branch account and reduces my profit, so I've no incentive to pass things freely. In the example you've just mentioned, I would say it's a business expense."

"Thanks very much, Henry. I promise I wont abuse the use of the card, though."

"No, I didn't think you would. You seem to be a responsible person." Henry stood up. "Did you enjoy your day here? It wasn't very busy, was it?"

"Yes, thanks. I've found it all most interesting and was glad to have a quiet first day to learn the ropes!"

"Glad to hear it! I'm leaving now. Make sure you lock the door when you leave at five."

Simon wandered around trying to concentrate on clearing up the office. His immediate thoughts took him to the idea of using his credit card to lease a car, so he looked up the number for the Ford dealership where he had spoken with Sally Field. She had seemed very helpful and willing to give him lessons, although she had been a difficult person to contact. He waited patiently for the phone to be answered and his heart missed a beat when he heard Sally's voice.

"Oh, hi!" he began, tentatively, "this is Simon Lightward. I met you once when I was looking for cars. Do you remember?"

"Oh, yes, I remember! You wanted a car before you could drive!" she replied with a chuckle. "How can I help you now?"

"Well I now have a credit card and would like to lease a vehicle; when could I come to se you?"

"Why don't you call here about 7 o'clock this evening? I'm sure we can find you something suitable."

"Okay, I'll be right along!" Simon joyfully hung up and set about locking the office

*   *   *   *

At home that evening he found his sister in the living room with a young man. She introduced her brother and he stood up to shake hands. "I'm glad to meet you, Simon! My name is Sandy MacNeil."

"Good lord! I've just started work for Sutherland and McNeill. Are you a relative?"

"How do they spell the last name? It's probably different from mine."

"M-C-N-E-I-L-L"

"Ah! It's not the same. But what do you do there, laddie?" asked Sandy.

Simon laughed. "Make the tea, mostly, it seems! - But I'm a trainee financial advisor and have to learn all about stocks and shares and the financial market in general."

"Hey! When I get started as a fully qualified doctor, I'll have to consult you about what to do with all my wealth!" There was an underlying Scots accent when Sandy spoke which made his voice sound attractive.

Samantha chipped in and said, "I've never known Dad to have so much money that he needed advice about investing it! I shouldn't get too hopeful, Sandy!"

Simon was curious about the relationship between his sister and Sandy. She had several different boy friends to his knowledge but this was the first she'd brought home. He walked over to where she was sitting. "How did you come to meet?" he asked quietly.

"At the hospital," she replied at once, "He's a new intern and we seemed to hit it off from the beginning. Do you like him?"

"He seems a pleasant fellow. I like his Scots accent!"

She smiled up at him with a twinkle in her hazel eyes. "And I like his red hair!"

Father came home from his day at the office, still formally attired, and addressed them all by saying, "My God! What a surprise finding my whole family – and, may I assume – future son-in-law together in one place!"

Samantha went over to Sandy and led him to her father. "Dad, this is Sandy McNeil. He's a new intern at the hospital but I wouldn't assume any implications, just because I've brought him home today!"

Doctor Lightward shook Sandy's hand. "I suppose I should call you doctor, too! What's your speciality?"

"I'm going into paediatrics and hope to establish a practise in Waterloo, when I fully qualify."

"Well, good luck to you, son! God knows we need more of your type today."

Mother came in and clapped her hands. "Everyone to the dining room for dinner," she announced. "It's on the table now and getting colder by the minute, so move it!"

CHAPTER SEVEN

The "Gang", to which Simon was party, met at their favourite Pub on Wednesday evening. The gathering had been called by Roy Helwig since he was the most organized of the group. Simon was the first to arrive, followed by Terry Wong, who asked, "Is everyone expected?"

"Well, No! Gerry said he had to work the evening shift and wouldn't be free till midnight."

"As he's a night auditor, I guess it limits his freedom," noted Simon.

"Then, if he can't join us, maybe we should consider visiting him when we've finished here?" Suggested Roy.

Vernon Spreitzer joined them at the table and asked if they'd ordered.

"No, we haven't, but as last to arrive, I suggest you do that for us all!"

"Bloody hell! I can't afford to pay for you guys. I'll order and you each pay your share!" He looked around for a waitress. "Where's Gerry, by the way?"

"He's working." Explained Simon. "But Ray suggested we all visit him later. What d'yer think?"

There was full agreement and orders were placed for drinks and chicken wings.

Simon relaxed back in his chair and studied his companions. It was hard to remember them back in University as they had become so much more mature. Sometimes he wondered whether their 'Gang' meetings became too boisterous or rowdy when they let themselves go but he knew it was a way of relieving tensions. Roy seemed to take everything in his stride, however. He was the sketch artist at school and had entered a career in architecture without delay. Looking at him now, Simon noted the long sleeved white dress shirt with a knotted red scarf around his neck and his face surmounted by a shock of curly black hair. He knew he was wearing green corduroy trousers and thought him the epitome of an artist.

Vernon, on the other hand appeared to be just what he was – an apprentice engineer. He wore a black tee shirt and well-worn blue jeans supported by a leather belt fitted to hold accessories needed on the job. His long open face was surmounted by his brown hair which was always kept very short.

"Heh, Vernon, why do you always look so satisfied?" Simon asked.

"Because I'm happily married and enjoy my work" said Vernon.

"Well, good for you. Later on, tell us how it happened!"

Finally, Simon turned his gaze on Terry. He had a typical roundish face of a person of Asian decent with straight black hair and slightly elongated eyes as if he was constantly squinting. He was a quiet fellow and smiled a great deal. Simon sometimes wondered if that was to conceal his true feelings but he liked him as a friend.

When the orders came there was friendly bantering and an exchange of news. Simon told of his appointment and Vernon proudly announced that he'd done a heating installation on his own and added, "I know that sounds good but it keeps me out late and my wife complains."

"Hope the damned thing works!" Chided Roy. "I wouldn't let you loose on one of my creations!"

"Huh! I doubt your building would stand long enough to be heated!" Vernon scoffed back.

"I need to go to the rest room," announced Terry.

"Probably, too many weird herbs!" said Simon. "I'll come with you though."

In the rest room they were the only ones present so they exchanged a few ribald remarks. Simon was conscious that Terry was taking a long time and seemed to have difficulty in adjusting his clothing and zipping his pants. He was jigging up and down.

"No matter how much you shake and dance, you'll always get some on your pants!" Simon said jokingly.

Terry responded with a loud laugh but was serious as he explained, "No, my zip tag is hard to get hold of when I push it down fully. I don't have trouble with my water works!"

They returned to the table and found the other two laughing loudly. Roy explained that he'd been asked to prepare drafts for some permanent notices in a building his firm was designing and misunderstood his directions. "I thought my boss said 'Do a couple for steaming vents', so I prepared a suggestion for a curved funnel with wavy lines coming out. When he saw them he laughed his head off and explained that what he said was 'Females and Gents'. He thought the men would have a job peeing through a curved funnel!"

"You should've been with me in the washroom when Terry had trouble with his zipper! My comment might also make you laugh! Ask Terry to explain it!" Said Simon.

When the chicken wings were gone and no one fancied another beer, Roy stood up and asked, "Who's coming with me to wake up old Gerry?"

"Just a minute," exclaimed Simon, "I've got some news for you!"

The group paused in the positions they had achieved as they started to stand up at Roy's suggestion and Vernon asked, "So, what's your news, Simon?"

"I've signed up to lease a new car!" Simon explained with pride.

They all spoke at once and Vernon asked, "When're we going to do see it?"

"When I get it, in a few days." answered Simon.

Terry said, "Never mind that! Let's stop at MacDonald's and get Gerry a whopper burger. He must be starving if he's been on duty since seven and missed his chicken wings!"

"Good idea," exclaimed Vern, "We'll get a Coke as well." There was complete agreement to this and they left the pub to catch a bus to the Holiday Inn.

On the journey they planned how to approach Gerry. It was finally agreed that Roy would go to the counter alone and ask for a room. The others would sit in the entry lobby to see Gerry's response, then they would improvise their moves. Before entering the Hotel they had bought the MacDonald's food and drink from a nearby outlet.

Fortunately, the Hotel lobby was empty that late in the evening so Roy went straight up to the counter. There was no one to be seen, so he rang the bell. Gerry popped out from a room at the back, looking very smart in a dress shirt covered by a waistcoat of navy blue. He approached Roy with his usual cheery smile.

"Good evening, sir. How may I help you?" Then his mouth gaped open as he recognized who it was. "My God!" he exclaimed. "What on earth are you doing here?"

"Hello, Gerry, old fellow." Said Roy. "You remember it's 'Gang' night, so we thought we'd bring the lads to you as you were slaving away behind this counter?"

The others joined Roy at the counter and Vernon handed over the Burger and drink. "We thought you'd be hungry, missing the wings tonight, so we brought you this!"

"You needn't have done that," declared Gerry. "I get food in the back there every night."

"Then save it for breakfast, old chum! We'd hate to waste it as it was brought here at great expense!" Simon explained. "You're looking very smart," he added. "Are you enjoying this job?"

"Thank you, Simon. I know I got this position because of you and I'm so grateful. This is a great firm to work for and I love my contacts with the public."

Gerry began to get restless as he kept peering back over his shoulder to the room behind the counter or the corridor to his right. "Look, you fellows! It's jolly decent of you to visit me like this but I don't like to have a crowd of you hanging around in case the manager shows up."

"We could all be on legitimate business," said Roy "Why don't you book us a room?"

"Would you all share if I gave you a double bedded room?" Gerry asked seriously.

"You won't get me sharing a room with these guys!" shouted Simon as he stepped away from the group.

"And we wouldn't sleep with a quasi-limey!" said the others almost in unison.

A middle-aged man in a blue suit appeared from the back room. "Do you need any help, Gerry?" he asked quietly.

"No. It's okay, sir," Gerry replied. "These gentlemen are just leaving. We haven't anything to suit them." He glared at his friends and they shuffled away towards the entrance. "Thank you for your enquiry, gentlemen! I hope to see you another day!"

CHAPTER EIGHT

It had been several weeks since Simon first went to work for Henry Allbine. He had absorbed the office routine and familiarized himself with the use of the computer to get trading activities from head office. He had become knowledgeable about regular clients who came in for consultation and advice but had never sat in on an interview. Imagine his surprise one morning when he read an e-mail message on the computer on his desk.

"Hi, Simon! I'm not well! Mr Ahmid Singh has an appointment with me for 11 a.m. today. Call him to let him know I'm indisposed but offer to see him yourself. He knows his investments very well and will probably only give you some investment directions which I'm sure you can handle.

Hope to be back tomorrow.

Henry"

Simon read it twice and felt a nasty hollow feeling come into his stomach. At that moment he seemed totally inadequate to deal with a client. It was like the time he was thrown into a swimming pool and told to swim two lengths. He thought he would drown but realized he knew the fundamentals of swimming over-arm, so he struck out. Afterwards he was proud that he'd done two lengths and never feared the water again. Could it be like this now, with a client he did not know? Henry must have confidence in me, he reasoned.

He picked up the handset and looked for the phone number on the Roladex. Maybe Ahmid Singh would be out; or maybe he would prefer to speak only to Henry. Either way he'd be off the hook! He dialled and was answered after two rings.

"Hello!" he heard a suave cultured voice say. "Who are you calling?"

"Good morning, sir." Simon answered promptly. "This is Henry Allbine's office and I believe you have an appointment with him this morning?"

"Yes. At eleven o'clock. Is there a problem?"

"Yes, Henry is not well and won't be in the office today. He asked me to offer to help you if it was urgent." Simon held his breath.

"And who are you, may I ask?"

"My name is Simon Lightward and I'm Henry's personal assistant."

"In that case, Simon, I would welcome a chat with you. Henry has already spoken well of you and how quickly you've picked up the business." The line was silent for a moment while the client pondered. "Very well, Simon! I'll see you at eleven."

The phone went dead and Simon very slowly put the handset on the rest. He let out a long breath and flopped back in his chair. "What have I let myself in for?" he said to no one and immediately started to assemble in his mind the kind of information he should have at hand. He retrieved the file on Ahmid Singh from the storage drawers in the office, although he was aware that it contained very little significant information about a client except the initial signed agreement. He signed on to the Company computer and called up the client's record. At once he was overwhelmed by the diversity of Singh's portfolio. It was worth over $5,000,000 as a book value and appreciably more on the current market value. The range of investments was mind-boggling and Simon shook his head in despair as he imagined the conversation he might have with Ahmid Singh at eleven.

Just in case the client wished to make more investments, Simon called up a list of securities currently on the market and found himself swamped by the large array.

"Oh well! Jump into the deep end, again, Simon, and start swimming!" he thought.

He'd just finished brewing a carafe of coffee in the back room when he heard the office door open. He came out, to see a tall athletic looking gentleman of eastern appearance dressed in an expensive looking grey suit, smiling at him in the friendliest way.

"Good morning, Simon. I am Ahmid Singh and have an appointment with you." He held out his hand and Simon advanced to shake it.

"I don't know how much I can be of assistance, Mister Singh. I have looked at your record and know the size of your holdings."

"Never mind, young man! Let me tell you why I wanted to see Henry and you can decide whether or not you can help."

"That's very understanding of you, sir. Shall we go in to Henry's office?"

They walked into the adjacent office and Mister Singh carefully chose to sit in the client's chair. Simon was impressed by his respect for proper etiquette as he left the owner's chair free. "I've made some fresh coffee." He said before sitting. "Would you like some?"

Mister Singh waved a hand from side to side. "Oh, No. No. No! I only drink tea!" He said softly. "and I don't want you to make some just for me."

Simon sat down feeling this man was so gentle and respectful that he dared not get himself the coffee he so desperately needed at that moment. "Now. How can I help you?" he said, looking straight into the client's brown eyes.

"I think I would like to tell you about my business, first, so you can have an appreciation of where I'm coming from." He gave Simon an indulgent smile as if speaking to a child. "Please understand that I am not suggesting you would not know how to help me but Henry and I have spoken so often over the years that he knows just where I stand."

"That's fine," Simon replied. "It's kind of you to spare the time to bring me up to speed." He sat back in his chair prepared to be attentive.

"I'm an entrepreneur! I'm told you went to London School of Economics, so you'll have a pretty good understanding of what that means." He gave Simon a wide smile displaying a perfect mouth of white teeth before continuing. "I don't have any stores or warehouses because I seek out a range of products and I organize their dispatch directly to the retail companies I deal with. This keeps overheads to a minimum and I never have unsold stocks on my hands." He waved his hands around again before explaining. "You see I don't BUY anything. I'm an agent who secures goods that companies tell me they need and take a commission when the goods reach the retail outlet. Do you follow?"

Simon understood the process as it had been discussed in college, so he simply nodded his head.

"Good! – I was told you were very bright! - So, when deals are closed and I receive the commission, I have a lot of money on my hands! This is why I'm here today, Simon."

"Umm! Can I ask how much you're wanting to invest right now?" Simon said sheepishly.

"Yes. I have one hundred and twenty-four thousand. I want you to invest it in the proportions that Henry and I have agreed previously. Do you have that information?"

Simon turned to the computer alongside him and studied the account details for Ahmid Singh. "Yes, it's here on record." He picked up a notepad and pen so he could write as he spoke. "You want twenty percent in grade A commercial bonds, the same proportion in Government securities, and the rest in high quality trust funds. Is that right?"

"Certainly, Simon. It's a rather safe kind of spread but, when I want the money, I like to know it will be there!" He chuckled in a good natured way.

"I can arrange suitable investments and check with you on the phone to see that you agree. Is that convenient, sir?" Simon hoped Henry would be back so he could run his choices past him tomorrow.

"That's quite suitable to me, young man! I'm going away next week, so please have this done before I go."

"Oh, yes! I shall be able to call tomorrow. Are you leaving a cheque with me to cover the investments, or will you let us have it when you've approved them?"

"No. I'll leave you a cheque now. It'll save me coming in again." He stood up and Simon followed. In the reception office they shook hands and Ahmid Singh left without another word.

Simon hurried into the back room to grab his much-needed coffee. He couldn't prevent himself from smiling as he reflected on the important piece of business he'd just concluded. He sat at his own desk and began the process of choosing securities to meet his client's need. With some modest arithmetic juggling he came up with a possible portfolio. He started to think about Singh's business and how much total sales value he must have shipped to give him $124,000 in commissions. Assuming twenty percent he would have despatched $620,000. The scale of his activities amazed Simon.

He was disturbed when a young woman entered the office. He stood up. "Good morning, ma'am. How can I help you?" He thought she looked about thirty and was very slim, dressed in a colourful top and blue jeans.

She smiled at him and said, "I've just come into an inheritance and I'd like advice about what to do with it."

Simon's first thoughts were that he could give her several ideas about what to do with her inheritance but he politely said, "Henry Allbine, the financial advisor, is away sick today. Would you like to explain to me what your general intentions are?"

She laughed. "I assume you mean intentions with regard to the inheritance, not things in general?"

"Well! We could discuss those too!" His heart was beating furiously as he asked, "How about dinner with me tonight?"

She did not step back in shock or show disapproval on her face but, instead, answered, "How about we talk investments first? Then I'll answer your question!"

"Yes, that would be wise. Sorry if I was out of line just then." He blushed and added, 'Please take a chair and tell me your problem."

"I'm the only surviving relative of my Aunt Matilda. In her will she made me sole executrix and sole beneficiary. I really don't know the procedures to enact the will and, when I realize all the assets, how do I get the money legally transferred to me?"

"Have you spoken to a lawyer?"

"No, I haven't. A friend of mine said it would be expensive."

"I see!" Simon peered at her intently and marvelled at her lovely face. He planned to keep her as a client, at least. "Tell me what you know of your Aunt's estate. Did she own her house; had she bank accounts or investments?"

"Yes, the house is in her name but I've been living with her for two years now – a sort of 'live-in' companion. I would really like to keep it, if I can – and oh, yes! - She had one bank account and two or three GIC's"

"This sounds quite straightforward." nodded Simon. "Have you any idea of the total value of her estate?"

His client put a finger to her lips and glanced at the ceiling. "At a quick estimate, I'd guess $250,000 for the house and $80,000 in GIC's."

Simon smiled at her gestures and said, "I think, with more than $300,000 you may have to file probate but I'll check with Henry."

"Do I need a lawyer for that?"

"I just don't know. I've never had to deal with an estate before but I'll phone you tomorrow as soon as I've briefed Henry." He smiled at her and suddenly remembered he hadn't asked her personal details. "I'm sorry, I haven't asked your name!"

She gave him a wide smile of gleaming white teeth. "I was wondering if you'd get to that!"

"Just let me get out a form," he said reaching into a drawer of the desk. "As you might have guessed, there'd be a form to fill out!"

She laughed. "My name is Francesca Mourie." She spelled it out and added, "I live at 25, Christopher Drive, Waterloo."

Simon wrote this down on his form and completed it with the Postal Code and telephone number. Then he asked her to sign as an acknowledgement that she undertook to be a client. When this was completed they both stood up and Simon asked again, "Will you have supper with me tonight! Say seven o'clock?"

She gave a warm smile as she agreed. "And will you pick me up?"

"Of course! I'm afraid I don't have a car yet as I'm awaiting delivery, so I'll choose a restaurant within walking distance!" They shook hands and Francesca nodded her agreement and then left with Simon in a daze.

CHAPTER NINE

Next morning, when Simon went to tell Henry about Ahmid Singh's proposed list of investments, his mind was not securely fixed on that business. He had had a delightful evening with Francesca and would rather tell Henry about her needs instead.

"How did you get on with our client?" Henry asked initially.

"Oh, really well! She was absolutely charming!" replied Simon, beaming from ear to ear.

"SHE?" questioned Henry. "Didn't you see Ahmid Singh?"

Simon quickly gathered his thoughts. "Of course I did! I just couldn't get Francesca out of my mind! – She came in after."

"Well, let's start with Ahmid's request. Have you prepared a list of recommended investments?"

"Yes, sir. Here it is." Simon passed over a neat list he'd written on paper.

"My! That guy certainly makes money, whatever he does!" Observed Henry.

"Yes, it made me wonder whether there was any drug smuggling involved in his activities."

"I don't think so, Simon. He's always been straight with me." He handed the list back to Simon and told him to call Ahmid and get approval. "Now, young man what's this about Francesca?"

"Well, she's a new client who has inherited money and needs help on how to proceed."

"Did you get her to sign our contract form?"

"Certainly! I didn't want to let her escape!"

"I'm glad you used your initiative on that, although I suspect you had deeper motives?"

Simon laughed, "Yes, you're right! I took her out to supper last night!"

Henry frowned and said very firmly, "You know it's a rule not to have personal relationships with clients?"

"Oh, no!" Simon exclaimed. "I've invited her out tonight, as well. Should I call it off?"

Henry was pensive when he recommended, "Get her to come in to see me, so that she becomes my client, then it may be okay for you, as assistant, to continue to see her."

"Oh, thanks, Henry! Shall I ask her to come in today?"

"Make it for two o'clock."

Henry had two clients to see that morning and Simon answered many phone calls and received several faxes which needed his attention.

He was happy when two o'clock came and Francesca appeared at the door. When he'd phoned her earlier he'd explained about the Financial Advisor not having personal relationships with a client and she was not the least concerned about the rule. She was looking delightfully fresh in a floral printed dress that just touched her knees and a pair of blue sandals. Her blond hair shone and her blue eyes sparkled. He jumped up and kissed her.

"Let's go and meet Henry," he said. "Don't think it'll take long!" He knocked on the door, opened it, and ushered Francesca in.

Henry stood and shook hands with her. "Welcome Miss Mourie. Please sit down." He turned to Simon. "Bring in another chair, please, Simon. I'd like you to stay."

Once they were settled, Henry asked about her circumstances and she gave the same information she'd given Simon the previous day. "Have you got a certified copy of the will?" he asked.

"She frowned and asked, "Certified by whom?"

"Well, usually a lawyer! If you've got the will with you, let me see it?"

She fumbled in her purse and pulled out a slim legal-sized envelope which she handed to Henry. "This is just as I found it in my Aunt's desk. She'd always told me where she kept everything."

Henry pulled out the two-page document and scanned it quickly. "It's a very simple will," he declared. "it's witnessed by two people. Do you know if they're alive?"

"Oh, yes!" Francesca replied cheerfully. "They're the next door neighbours. I asked them in when my Aunt made her will only a few months ago."

Henry applied a rubber stamp to the last page and signed it. "There you are," he said, handing the document back to her. "It's certified!"

"Oh, thank you! I was afraid I was going to have to get an expensive lawyer!" She graced Henry with an especially long warm smile.

He gave her a nod. "Now, take that, with the death certificate, and the GIC's to the bank that issued them and they will transfer them to your name." He paused, frowning. "Why did your Aunt have a different last name from you?"

"She married a man from Australia but he died before they had any children. In later life she reached out to me for companionship, as the only other relative."

"Thank you. I asked because banks are less suspicious if the transfer is to the same last name!" He peered at her intently and added, "I wouldn't rush to transfer title to the home so it doesn't raise any question of capital gains, but let the City know you'll pay the tax bills!"

Francesca stood and shook his hand. "You've been such a help, Mister Allbine. It's made everything so simple!" As she reached the door she gave a sideways suggestive smile and said, "So it's okay to go on dating Simon?"

He laughed and turned to Simon. "You're just a lucky fellow to have met this lovely young lady! Treat her right!"

Simon grabbed Francesca's hand and drew her out to his office where they exchanged a quick kiss. "See you at seven?" She nodded and skipped away.

When Simon got home that afternoon, he found Samantha in the kitchen admiring a beautifully carved wooden box which she'd just unwrapped.

"What've you got there?" asked Simon as he peered closely at it.

"It's a jewellery casket I bought from the market." She lifted the lid and showed him a divided lift-out tray. "This is for all my earrings, rings and brooches and, underneath, I can keep necklaces or bracelets."

Simon took it from her. "It's very beautifully finished and will be useful now you've got a boy friend who'll shower you with gifts!" He handed it back. "What's this white stuff in the corners at the bottom?"

She peered at it intently and tried to blow the dust out. "Hmm! Doesn't seem to want to shift. Maybe it's something they used to polish the inside?" She tried to move the white marks from the corners and edges with her finger nail. A little came off and she tested it with her tongue. "Tastes like some drugs I've used – like marijuana or cocaine!"

"Did you get it from one of those small lock-up shops in the market?" asked Simon.

"Yes. I think it was called 'Far East Frivolities'. You know, stuff from Indonesia, Korea, and such places."

"Look! I'm going out with my new girl friend, Francesca, this evening. Just out of curiosity we'll have a look at their goods and see if others have any white powder. If we do find more, I suggest you take your box back for a refund. You don't want to risk any chance that it's a drug."

"Thanks, Simon. That's good of you! I hope you'll bring Francesca home so we can meet her!"

"I sure will! She's a real corker!"

Simon picked up Francesca at seven and asked if she liked Chinese food. She said she loved it so he drove them to a place on King Street. They had to park in a lot off the main street but it was a warm evening and they didn't mind the short walk. On the way, Simon asked if Francesca minded if they dropped in at the market after supper. He explained about the white powder in Samantha's jewellery box.

"That's okay by me! I love looking around unusual market stalls."

"Good. That'll save me moving the car as we're not far away from the market."

They reached the restaurant and were seated at a secluded table in a booth decorated with bamboo screens and painted flowers. The waitress took their order and quickly returned with tea for each of them.

"I do like the kimonos the waitresses wear here. They're so gorgeously decorated with embossed silks and gilt thread." Francesca remarked as she followed the waitress with her eyes.

"They look so elegant, too!" agreed Simon, "the way they seem to glide everywhere!"

"I wish I was more elegant," complained Francesca, "I've never had much opportunity to learn deportment and dressing."

"I see nothing wrong in you! You attracted me the moment you walked into the office!" He studied her carefully and noticed how her blond hair was styled short but curving towards the front of her ears. Her eyes were a bright blue and her skin an unblemished delicate pink. She wore a simple blue blouse with a turned back collar but an unbuttoned open neck. He remembered that her skirt only touched the top of her knees and was a royal blue. Finally he said, "You are beautiful and tastefully dressed!"

"No! I've got none of the graces of the high born! I come from a very working class family who never had much money and always dressed very casual. I don't remember seeing Dad in a collar, tie and a jacket, even to go to a funeral!"

"Wasn't your Aunt Matilda in a different position? She seemed to have a bit of money."

"She was! She had her own standards and I learned a lot from her. She knew how to dress for every occasion and had good taste and manners."

"So, she understood social form?" asked Simon.

Francesca could not reply at that moment because the waitress brought their chosen dishes. They each took a while to survey the delicious food and load their plates. Conversation lapsed to intermittent comments about their food until they were almost finished.

"Going back to what you said about my Aunt, I believe she did understand the formalities of society, although where she got it from, I don't know. I never heard my parents talking about her side of the family. She was my Dad's sister, of course, but she lived alone in another city until she got married. What happened during her few married years I never heard tell."

"Never mind. You'll find I'm obsessed with form, especially the paper ones which I'd love to burn up in a massive bonfire!"

Francesca laughed and said, "You'll never win that one. Look at Guy Faulkes in England who tried to blow up the Houses of Parliament!"

"Shall we go?" asked Simon, "before I explode in another way!" He paid the bill at the desk and they left to walk to the market.

The original outdoor market had been covered over by a permanent structure some years back and the entrance was made by mounting a few steps from the sidewalk. When they pushed through the doors they were aware of a bustle of activity in the aisles although it was not a market day. That only meant that the farmers were not present with their fresh produce but the permanent stalls and shops were open for business. Simon and Francesca wandered around trying to locate the premises where his sister had bought the jewellery box. They spotted it in one corner and did not need to confirm the name because the whole front of the shop was covered by hanging baskets, ornaments, decorative carvings and artificial flowers.

"This is marvellous!" Francesca declared. "I'm going to have a good look round while you locate the box like the one your sister bought."

"Okay! Meet out front in fifteen minutes?" Simon said this as he squeezed past her to enter the inside of the shop.

He picked up several carved wooden boxes one after another and couldn't find one that matched his sister's. Seeing a man standing in the rear of the displays he went up to him. As he got close, he couldn't decide whether the man was Egyptian or pale East Indian, but he was handsome and wore a Nehru jacket with matching pants.

"Excuse me, sir," he said. "I am looking for a carved box with an inner tray. It must measure about twelve by eight by four. Have you anything like that you could show me?"

The man smiled and shook his head. "I'm afraid I sold the last one of those earlier today. I can show you several in different sizes."

"That's okay." Simon said as he walked away, his mind made up that he would carefully examine a smaller one. He had looked at it previously but, this time, he took out the tray. Sure enough, there were traces of white powder and it smelled of some sort of drug. For some moments he pondered over what he should do and, finally, decided to tell Samantha to return the box if she was in any doubt.

He left the inside of the shop and found Francesca waiting for him.

"You took your time, Simon! I was about to come in and rescue you!"

"I had to ask the shopkeeper for a box of the size Samantha bought but he had no others like it. One of the smaller ones I looked in did have white powder, though."

"So? What're you going to do?"

"I'm going to suggest she returns the one she bought. I don't see what else is open to us."

"Then let's go home! Will you stay with me tonight?"

Simon was aghast at her suggestion but saw no reason not to accept her invitation. "I've no overnight stuff with me, does that matter?"

Francesca squeezed his arm. "No! Of course not, silly! I want you as you are!"

CHAPTER TEN

As Simon drove Francesca to her home, he had some misgivings about her unexpected invitation for him to stay the night. He certainly found her attractive and felt very relaxed in her company. She was bright and intelligent but she had not revealed much of her past except for the pieces she gave him over supper. He was not the kind of person who would expect to go to bed with a woman on only their second date; it did not seem to be proper form, and it made him wonder about her standards.

When they stopped at her front entrance he asked, "Do you really want to do this? Shouldn't we get to know one another better?"

Francesca turned to face him squarely, her eyes glistening from the reflection of the street lights. "I know myself and I've got good feelings about you. I think we'd get to know each other better by spending the night in bed! I'm not asking for a long term relationship unless it turns out to be our mutual desires!"

"Okay! You've made it clear what your intentions are! So, I'm happy to go along!"

They joined hands and mounted the steps to the door which she opened.

There was a long hallway leading to the kitchen at the back of the house. Stairs branched up to the right and to the left a door opened into a sitting room. Francesca led the way in and switched on lights.

Simon noticed a marble fireplace surround on the far wall with two leather armchairs positioned on either side and behind the one farthest from the window stood a floor lamp of modern design.

"This is very nice," complimented Simon as he chose to sit in that particular chair.

"Thank you, Simon, but I can't take credit for the décor. It was all done by my Aunt before I came to live here." Francesca walked over to what Simon thought was a bookcase with a dropped front but, when she opened the front, he saw it was full of liquor bottles. "Would you like a drink?" she asked.

"Some scotch and water, if you have it!"

She prepared the drink and brought it to him in a crystal cut glass. "There you are! I hope I've judged the water right?"

Simon took a sip and nodded his head. "Perfect, thanks"

She returned to the cabinet and poured something for herself. Simon couldn't guess whether it was gin or vodka. She carried it to the other chair, sat down, and said, "I propose a toast! May we embark on a long and satisfying relationship?" She took a sip and smiled at Simon.

He raised his glass and said, "I concur! Cheers!"

And this proved to be the beginning of a very satisfying night, if nothing else!

*   *   *   *

When Simon returned to his parent's home the following evening after work, His mother immediately asked him, "And where were you last night?"

"I stayed with my girl friend, Francesca. She's inherited a house from her Aunt."

"Well, I hope you know what you're doing. I suppose you slept with her?"

Simon felt angry at this inquisition. "I don't see what business it is of yours. I'm a fully fledged adult, y'know?"

Their conversation came to an end when Samantha came into the kitchen carrying a wrapped parcel. She set it down on the table and threw her purse on a chair before acknowledging Simon. "Oh, hello Simon! I'm glad you're here. I've changed that box you saw to something smaller but clear of white powder."

"I'm glad you did, Sis. I went to the shop last night and the proprietor didn't have any others like the one you bought but I examined some of the smaller ones and they did have powder in them, so I'm glad you've got a clean one."

"It took some time to find a clean one but here it is!" She unwrapped the box and everyone peered inside to check it was clean. "But I took a few scrapings from the original to our laboratory and the manager promised to analyse it when he's got time."

Father came in, noticed Simon, and said, "So! The prodigal son has returned!"

"Don't you start!" shouted Simon. "I've had enough questions from Mum."

"I only asked where he spent the night," complained Mother.

"Where were you anyway?" Asked Samantha.

"As I said to mother, it's none of anybody else's business but I slept with my girl friend!"

She laughed along with father who commented. "He really is growing up!"

"Look, sis, when you get the results from your hospital lab, let me know, would you? If it's drugs, I have a suspicion about where they came from." Simon said.

"Oh! Are you going to tell us your suspicions?" Samantha joshed him.

"Not now! It's far too premature. I've got to do a bit of sleuthing first."

"Why can't we just take it to the police?" asked father.

"Because it'll all get complicated and we might come under suspicion. They might think that you, being a doctor, are trying to cover up something you've done, for example."

"Huh! Your imagination is carrying you away!" He waved his hands dismissively. "More important, right now, is when can I get the help you promised to work on computerizing my records. I've hired a guy that says he's done this for others, so I would just like you to talk to him before he gets into planning my system."

Simon frowned and looked straight at his father. "I don't know when I could be free in the daytime, Dad. Any chance this guy could come over one night when we can see him together?"

"Oh, I guess so. I'll phone him tomorrow and make a date."

Mother asked out loud, "It's nice to have all the family home for supper but will you leave my kitchen so I can serve everything up?"

Without comment they all went into the dining room. Father said he must go and wash his hands before he sat down while Samantha checked on her appearance in a mirror before saying, "Well, I washed my hands before leaving the Hospital with that special germicidal guck, but I'm real hungry!"

"Did you get lunch in the cafeteria?" said Simon and added, "I didn't have time to eat today. I had to live on coffee. There was a heck of a lot of activity in the stocks."

"Did your girl friend give you breakfast this morning?"

"She did, as a matter of fact," answered Simon. "She's a terrific cook!"

"I'm glad to hear it! I wish I was a decent cook. If Sandy and I get married, we'll probably live on frozen foods except for the ghastly porridge he loves for breakfast!"

Mother came in with hot dishes and set them on the table. Now, where's Dad got to? I don't want the food getting cold!"

He came in at that moment but before seating himself he said to Simon, "I've called my computer guy and he'll come over tomorrow evening. Okay by you?"

"It should be, Dad. We should get it over with quickly."

Then everybody tucked into their supper with relish.

*   *   *   *

Simon called Francesca on the phone next morning and explained his commitment to help his father with computerising his records which meant that he would not see her that night.

"That's okay, my love! I know you have a life of your own so we'll get together as often as possible."

"So glad you understand, dearest! I shall miss you, though!"

"Me, too! Shall I see you tomorrow night?"

"Wouldn't miss it for the world!"

He was busy all day with Henry Allbine due to the activity on the stock exchange so he was delayed in arriving home for supper. The family had finished eating but his mother had saved a meal in the oven. "You'd better eat it up quickly, Simon! Dad's already in his office with the computer guy."

Simon did just that and bounded up the stairs two at a time. "Sorry I'm late, Dad! Busy at work."

"Never mind! Come and meet David Balster!" Doctor Lightward moved toward the visitor who stood up from sitting in front of the computer.

Simon extended his hand. "Nice to meet you. Have you made much progress yet?"

David shook Simon's hand vigorously and his face lit up with enthusiasm. "Yes, we are getting along famously." He had a high pitched voice with a precise diction. "But we are glad you have come to help us."

The Doctor moved chairs around to allow Simon to sit and view the computer. When they were all settled David spoke again.

"I have brought a demonstration program to exemplify the principles of the system the Doctor could use to have all his records on computer." He paused to look at each of the other two men sitting alongside him. "We have already installed my system in 23 offices and have good responses from the users." He drew himself upright and touched a few keys lightly. "Now, here you see our main screen containing the basic information about the patient. It contains no medical details."

The two men peered at the screen and the Doctor asked, "So where do you keep the medical information? I hope it's secure?"

"Of course," answered David in a somewhat superior tone, "It's another screen and can only be accessed after entering a password." He demonstrated this on the computer.

The form listed a number of codes which meant nothing to Simon but his Father said "Ah! The Ontario Medical Association's classification of procedures?"

"Exactly," replied David. "From this you can have a comprehensive record of what has happened to each patient and use it for billing the Government."

"What about presenting symptoms when a patient first arrives?" asked the Doctor.

Simon stood up suddenly. "Look, you guys seem to know what you're doing. I don't think you need me."

"Do you want to get away to your girl friend?" asked his father with a smirk.

"Sure, if you don't mind. We can talk over any questions in your mind at another time."

"Go ahead, son! You've kept your promise to help, so go and enjoy yourself!"

Simon skipped out of the room with only a wave to David and rushed out to his car to drive to Francesca.

CHAPTER ELEVEN

They had a lovely night together and, lying side by side in bed the next morning, Simon wished it could be forever. Reluctantly he stirred as he knew he must get to work but Francesca stayed him by holding one arm. "Hang on a minute, darling, I want to talk to you."

Simon swung his legs back into bed. "You sound very serious. Are you going to tell me not to come again?"

"No, silly! I'm running short of money. I don't think I can pay this month's electricity bill and taxes."

"My God! I'd no idea you were in that situation." He turned to look directly into her blue eyes which he saw were misty with tears.

"What's happened?"

The tears welled forth and she grabbed the edge of the sheet to dab them. "I thought my Aunt received monthly income from an endowment which automatically went into the bank account, so I just spent as we always did; charging the groceries and paying other small bills by credit card. When I paid those off there was nothing left in the account."

Simon put his arm around her shoulders. "We'll sort this out together. This evening I'll go through all the accounts since your Aunt died and figure out just what went wrong. Is that okay?"

Francesca nodded and gave him a kiss. "Yes! I knew you'd help me but I don't expect money from you. If necessary I will get a job."

"Of course, my love, don't you worry! I'll help you make a financial plan!" He got out of bed and went to shower. A moment later Francesca tapped on the door.

"Do you want some breakfast?"

"You bet!" he called back, "I can't work without food!"

Later that evening, as they were going through all the records, it became apparent that Francesca had not advised the organization that held the endowment for her Aunt, of her inheritance of it under the will. Since she had also changed the name of the bank account to her own, the direct deposit of the monthly endowment had never reached any account. Together, they prepared a letter to correct things and she was convinced that the month or two arrears of deposit of the endowment would provide sufficient to pay off the outstanding bills.

"So, you won't have to get a job after all?" suggested Simon.

She smiled. "Were you getting concerned that I might not be able to look after you as you expected?"

Simon gave a quick laugh. "No! Nothing like that. It's just that I saw Ahmid Singh this afternoon and he was complaining that he couldn't keep up with his record-keeping and needed some help!" He turned to give her a hug. "So, I immediately thought of you!"

"That's sweet of you, honey! But I don't quite know what I could do?"

Simon realized that he knew little of her earlier life before she came to care for her Aunt, so he asked, "What did you work at before coming here?"

Francesca laughed and answered, "Shop assistant, library assistant, dress maker, and clerk."

"My, you could be called 'well-rounded' couldn't you?"

"As long as you're not referring to my figure, I'd agree!"

Simon took her hand. "My love, you have the most perfect figure I've ever seen!"

"You always flatter me!" She withdrew her hand. "In all seriousness, Simon, what could I hope to do for Mister Singh?"

"Well, he mentioned record-keeping. You were a clerk at some time; don't you think you could help him out in that department?"

"Are you sure you're not pushing me to get a job?"

He laughed again. "Of course not! The only job I'd want for you is to be my wife!"

Francesca threw up her hands in mock horror. "Simon!" she exclaimed. "Is that a proposal?"

Simon blushed and hung his head, "Afraid not, sweetheart! I don't think we're at that point yet. I just wanted to draw your attention to the possible position Ahmid might have."

There was a brief silence between them when Simon wondered if he'd offended her, until she spoke again seriously. "How do I contact Mister Singh?"

"I can give you his name and address and a cell phone number. He paused to assess how serious she was. "Do you think you'll go through with applying for a position?"

"I don't see why not! I was thinking of getting a job before you mentioned this opportunity. Have you any objections?"

"Of course not, darling. I'm sure you could be of great help to our client."

"Tomorrow, then! I'll have a go!"

When Simon got back to her after work the following day, she greeted him with excitement, her eyes sparkling and her face alight with happiness. She pulled him inside quickly and said, "I've got the job!"

Simon gave her a kiss and hug, lifting her off the ground to whirl around in the hallway of her house. "How wonderful!" he exclaimed between breaths. "What will you be---doing? When will you ---start?"

"Put me down and I'll tell all!" Simon did that and she took his hand to lead him into the sitting room. She pushed him into an arm chair and sat on the arm crossed legged. "Mister Singh is *such* a gentleman and we had a long conversation during which he told me what he needed. It amounted to very straightforward keeping of records of supplies he'd ordered and to whom they were to be sent. When he asked whether I thought I could do that, I said it was just like records I'd kept at a warehouse where I'd worked before. He said I sounded like the perfect fit and hired me there and then!"

"Well, congratulations, darling. So, when will you start?"

"On Monday, of course! No point in wasting time!"

Simon pulled her onto his lap and caressed her thigh. "Now, to celebrate, I'm going to take you out for an unusual meal!"

"Really? Where're we going?"

"To the *Fish and Fiddle* to have chicken wings and beer!"

"Ouch! I've never heard of that before! How do you know I'll like it?"

"Oh, you've got to like it, 'cause you'll meet my four best chums!"

Francesca screwed up her face in disgust. "You call that a celebration? Sounds it'll be more like an inquisition for me!"

Simon stood up and kissed her. "I promise, it'll be fun!"

The gang were waiting for them at the Pub; Gerry, Roy, Terry and Vernon, sitting round a large table with glasses of beer in front of them. As Francesca and Simon entered they all cheered and the other patrons looked around in horror. Gerry stood up and shifted chairs around to make room for the newcomers. Then he gave Simon a hug and said, "Can I hug this lovely lady too?"

The others chorused "W_O_O!" and, when Gerry sat down again after his hug, Simon formally introduced Francesca. The others mumbled their welcomes as the newcomers took their seats.

Simon was next to Roy who quietly said to him, "You're a lucky fellow! How did you meet this beautiful maiden?"

"It was through my work. She was a client."

"I didn't think people in your job were allowed to have a personal relationship with a client?"

"Well, I didn't! My boss made her his client but I retained custodial rights!"

"Hey guys!" Roy spoke up. "didn't we say he was always a lucky fella? If he fell down a sewer he'd come up with a Mars bar!"

"Yeh! She's too good for you, Simon!" shouted Vernon as he turned to Francesca. "Don't you trust him, my girl! He'll only lead you into deep trouble with his English style of manners!"

Simon jumped in. "Ignore them all, Francesca! They're just jealous louts!"

She laughed aloud. "I think, in their way, they've given me a wonderful welcome to your gang!"

"Huh! Why would you think that?" asked Terry in his serious manner.

"Because all that joshing was because Simon was loved by you all and it showed your friendship."

Putting his arm around Francesca's shoulders, Simon said, "Isn't she smart as well as lovely?"

The others waved their hands at him and cried for him to shut up but he spoke over their protests. "No! Listen guys! I've got a strange mystery that I'd like you to help with." He watched the others until he had their full attention before he continued. "My sister bought a wooden box the other day and there was a white powder in one section. She changed the box for a clean one but, before she did that, she took samples of the powder to her lab at the hospital. I went to the store where she bought it from and other boxes had similar powder. She was told by the lab Manager that he analysed the powder to be cocaine or a mix of it with something else. I have a suspicion about how it came into the country but I need some help to do more sleuthing. Any volunteers?"

"Why don't you go to the police?" asked Roy.

"Because all I have is circumstantial and I think they would dismiss it."

Gerry intervened. "Remember, his Dad's a doctor and the police might think this is family trying to cover his tracks?"

The others laughed at the idea and Vernon said, "Well, I've no time. I'm already working overtime as it is."

"Nor have I" chorused the others.

"So it looks as if I'm on my own?" Simon sighed.

"No you aren't!" cried Francesca. "I'll help in any way I can."

There was a chorus of "Aaah!" and laughter broke out all round.

Simon said, "Fran! I promised you beer and chicken wings tonight. Let's order some before these hungry wolves eat the lot!"

CHAPTER TWELVE

The next evening, after work, Simon decided to visit home rather than going straight to Francesca. He particularly wanted to find out how his Father had got on with the patient record program.

When he entered the kitchen his Mother turned from the stove on which she had a pot boiling and wrapped her arms around him in a welcoming hug.

"Oh, how nice to see you, Simon, how are you?"

Simon kissed her cheek, pushed her gently away from him, and said, "Mum, you look ravishing. You seem to grow younger every time I see you!"

"Oh, Simon, don't you flatter me. I'm the same as ever but what about you?"

"I didn't answer your question, did I? Well, I'm perfectly fine and very happy!"

"I'm so glad, son. I was afraid you might have got into bad company when you stayed with that girl."

"Mum! I'm a big boy and you can trust me. "'That girl', as you called her, is an honest, intelligent and lovely person. I must bring her to see you some time soon."

"I'm so glad for you! Please bring her round."

Father came downstairs and joined them. "Who do you want him to bring round, Mother?"

"Why, this lovely girl friend, of course. Wouldn't you like to meet her, too?"

"Certainly, I would!" He moved over to Simon and clapped him on the shoulder. "You look good, m'boy! This girl friend must be looking after you well!"

"She certainly does, Dad! In fact I have ideas about moving in with her. If I did would I still have to give you the money I do now and would it cause you any difficulties?"

"Oh, more surprises!" complained his Mother. "No sooner is he back home than he wants to leave!"

"Now then, Mother," pleaded her husband. "He's only behaving as most young men do today. Off with the old and on with the new! I don't think we'll be financially embarrassed to lose your short-lived contribution but we'll miss you!"

"I won't mind," said his Mother, "if you promise to visit often - and with your lovely lady, too!"

Simon felt elated at their reception of his ideas but guilty that he hadn't broached the idea with Francesca first. He wondered what she might say. "This is wonderful of you to accept me leaving the comfort of home and I will visit often!"

"Well, come on your two! I'll have Samantha home soon and you'll all want supper! Let me get on!" cried Mother.

The two men walked into the sitting room and Simon thought this would be a good opportunity to quiz his Father about patient records.

"How did you get on with that computer guy after I left?"

His Father sat heavily in an arm chair. "We got along fine! I understood the model program he demonstrated and told him what I would like to see changed."

"I'm glad to hear it, Dad! So, when will you be able to bring it into operation?"

The Doctor sighed before answering. "I see that as the biggest problem. As I'm sure you know, I'll have to get all my patients' personal data entered and then convert the last few visits of each of them into the standard medical procedure coding." He sighed again. "You can imagine, that's a lot of work."

"Couldn't you hire a temp to do the first part and then start using the system to record medical information day by day as it occurred?"

"That's an idea!" agreed his Father, "but every time I saw a patient I'd have to have their paper file in front of me as well as updating their computer record."

"And that's exactly what we wanted to avoid! Away with forms!"

The Doctor laughed. "I know! It's a battle to get rid of the paper and save the trees!"

"But if you did what you're suggesting, after a year your medical records would be almost up-to-date, wouldn't they? Then you could ditch the old files."

"For a high proportion of my patients, I'd say you were right. Taking the longer term view it does seem possible."

"There y'go then!" exclaimed Simon. "Give it a try!"

His Father laughed again. "I find it amazing how the young think everything is possible! You're perpetual optimists! We older types are more cautious but more sure in the end!"

Mother entered the room with a steaming dish of food. "Come on, you two, sit up to table and eat!"

Samantha joined them and there was a lively conversation as they ate their meal as a family. When it was finished Simon told his sister of his intention to move out. She became very sarcastic and a battle of words ensued between them until Mother brought it to an end by telling Samantha to go to her room if she could not be more civil. Without a backward glance she did as she was told and Simon detected in her attitude that streak of jealousy in her that had long pervaded their relationship. Then Simon said goodbye to his parents and left for Francesca's home.

There were no lights on when he got there and no response to his knocking on the door. He was not surprised that she was out because he had told her he would be visiting his parents and staying for supper. Since she appeared to lack any friends he could hardly imagine where she had gone. Perhaps she had gone to a restaurant or fast-food place for her evening meal? He patrolled up and down the street for ten minutes but, as it became darker, he began to worry. He walked to the nearest bus stop and waited until one came but she was not on it. He had left his car parked on the street outside her home. He had collected it from the dealer only that morning so he decided to drive it to the mall, thinking she might be shopping there and then he could give her a ride home. However, when he returned to the street he saw a light in her window. His spirits lifted and he jogged to her door. Before he knocked Francesca opened it and greeted him with a passionate kiss.

"When I came home I couldn't imagine where you were." She said hurriedly

"Where were you?" demanded Simon belligerently.

"I went to the hairdressers, darling! Please don't be cross! I do have a life, y'know!"

Simon was angry with himself at his reaction but told himself it was because of concern for her safety. "I'm sorry, dearest. I spoke in haste! Can we go in and talk?"

Francesca had not realized that her precipitate greeting and subsequent words had all been done on the doorstep. "Oh! Sorry, my love! Come in and we'll do more than talk!"

"Is that a promise?" he asked, smilingly.

"Well see, shall we?" she answered with her salacious smile, as they went into the living room.

"Simon, let me explain! I thought you'd stay with your folks tonight and I wouldn't see you. So I took the opportunity to get my hair done."

"I must say that I was quite concerned that you were out but, now I've thought about it, I know you have every right to do what you must. We are two independent people who have become good friends and we don't have any control over, or responsibility for, one another."

"Aren't you forgetting the feelings we have for one another," asked Francesca. "Doesn't our love modify that cold statement you've just made?"

Simon felt exasperated. "Oh, you women! I shall never understand how you think!"

"So, do you agree with my question or not?"

"Yes, I do agree. It was my love for you that wanted me to rescue you from the wicked world you must have ventured into!" He stood up and drew her out of the chair, "Maybe this kiss will help you to believe me!" he whispered as they dissolved into one another's arms.

After they had settled their mild dispute Simon said, "By the way, Fran, I collected my new car this morning. Maybe you'd like to see it?"

"That's great, my love! It will be so much more convenient for you to get around."

"And both of us!" exclaimed Simon.

"Of course but you'll be the main user."

"So, do you want to see it?"

"Not now, darling. I'm rather tired and would sooner go to bed."

In bed together, later, Simon asked a tentative question. "Francesca, would you allow me to live here with you on a more or less permanent basis?"

She sat up suddenly. "Good heavens!" she exclaimed. "Are you making another proposal of marriage? You do have a strange way of going about it!"

Simon pulled her down against him. "Now don't get the wrong idea, sweetheart! I'm not averse to marrying you but over the next short while I would like to live here with you."

"I see," she murmured into his shoulder. "Can you tell me more of what is on your mind?"

"Yes! I've given it some thought!"

"I'll bet you have!" she answered quickly.

"Now, this is in all seriousness! I could have that third bedroom as my office and a place for my clothes. We could share the rest of the house and I could pay you $200 a month to go towards the cost of this place. That might help you out financially but the amount is negotiable within reason!"

"What reason?" she asked. "I have no idea whether that amount would cover all the extra costs of you living here and, presumably, eating here! I might want three times that amount knowing your appetite!" She hid her smile under the sheet as she said this.

"Well! Forget the financial side for the moment! How about the principle of me sharing this home with you?"

"Without getting married?" She giggled. "What would the neighbours say?"

"Oh, Francesca, please be serious for a moment. Don't you see that I love you so much that I want to be with you all the time?"

"And I love you so much that I'd be furious if you didn't come and live here!"

They laughed together and made love again while they were still in bed.

CHAPTER THIRTEEN

Ahmid Singh had been born in the Rajasthan Province of India in 1960 in a small town west of Delhi. His parents chose a wife for him when he was twelve. She was named Salina and they were married in 1982. To the dismay of both parents the marriage was barren but they had heard of treatments that were available in the West which might solve this problem. In 1990 they paid for the children to immigrate to Canada. Ahmid had a brother who was disowned by the parents because he joined a revolutionary group called the Taliban so that he moved to Pakistan near the border with Afghanistan. The brothers kept in touch, however, because Ahmid was very broad minded and believed that everybody should have the right to choose their religion or allegiances. He heard that his brother was involved in the poppy business and was becoming very wealthy. From time to time Ahmid helped his brother by travelling to other countries and negotiating the transport of poppy products. When he was established in Canada he continued to do this, as well as acting as an entrepreneur for himself, purchasing and selling manufactured products.

Some two years after coming to Canada Ahmid had enough money to make a down payment on a house in St. Agatha near the City of Waterloo. It was an old country stone-built home that was once owned by the farmer who worked the surrounding land. When he died, his family sold the farm land but left the house and modernized it before putting it on the market. When Ahmid and his wife saw it on one of their car trips they both expressed the desire to live there. They both felt that the quietness of the country would suit them, yet it was not far from the City for all their needs.

Ahmid's business continued to blossom and he accumulated a small fortune which he had invested with the help of Henry Allbine and, on this particular day, he was on his way to see him again. When he arrived at Henry's office he was out but his assistant was able to see him.

"Good morning, Mister Singh," Simon said shaking his hand. "How nice to see you again! Please sit down."

"Indeed, I am happy to see you, also, Simon," Ahmid replied as he carefully sat on an office chair. "I should have made an appointment with Henry so it is my fault that he is not in attendance but I am sure you can help me this time."

Simon noticed again how all his visitor's speech and actions were very precise.

"How can I help you this morning?" asked Simon.

"I am carrying a draft from my brother in Pakistan but it is denominated in rupees. Can I pay this into my account?"

"I don't know, offhand, but I'll enquire at our head office through the computer."

"Ah, yes! Wonderful machines, these computers! Alas, I have never mastered them and keep all my records in books!"

There was silence while Simon gave his attention to the computer monitor. Shortly he looked up and said, "I'm sorry but we can't accept a draft in rupees. I suggest you go to your bank first, covert it to Canadian dollars and then we can apply it to your account."

Ahmid Singh was thoughtful and finally said. "I see! I suppose I shall have to produce evidence that the drawer is genuine and the amount can be guaranteed?"

"More than likely," answered Simon, "probably you'll have more forms to sign or get authorised. Forms could be the death of us! It's a pity your brother didn't have his bank transfer it electronically."

"Is that possible?" asked Ahmid in surprise. "I have never heard of such a thing!"

"It's done all the time in business, especially when large amounts are involved. That way the transferor bank is sure that there are sufficient funds in the account to transfer. With the draft you have, you may have to get evidence of its certainty of payment or, if the Bank accepts it, have to wait several weeks before you can access the money."

"This is all very complicated for a simple man like me! Thank you for explaining things, Simon. I must be on my way, then. Goodbye!"

Simon watched him carefully fold his spectacles into a case, pocket the case, rise slowly from his chair and leave the office. He followed his progress through the window in the door speculating on the possibility of Ahmid's wealth coming from his brother as well as the man's own efforts.

At home with Francesca that evening, he mentioned his encounter with Ahmid Singh.

"Did he speak of me at all?" she asked.

"No. Did you ever tell him when you went for the job, that you and I were close?"

"Of course not! I just said I'd heard about the job through a friend."

"That's good! I don't want to make him suspicious in any way, in case we have to tackle him about the drugs my sister found."

"So, you think Ahmid may be involved in drug smuggling?"

"Oh! I don't know, Fran, but today he wanted to deposit money he said had come from his brother in Pakistan and we know that's close to Afghanistan where poppies are the biggest crop."

"Maybe Ahmid's not involved in the actual smuggling but his brother is and he just uses Ahmid's imports as a way of hiding the drugs?"

"I wonder, Fran! Could you look at his records as you're working with them to see whether anything strikes you as unusual or abnormal?"

"Sure I will! Right now I can't imagine what I'm looking for. It's early days for me so I haven't much feel for the record process but I'll keep it in mind."

"Thanks, darling! Just be careful, won't you. I don't want to lose you now we've got together!"

The next day was Saturday and Francesca announced that she was going to her keep-fit classes. Simon decided to call Gerry to see if he was free for the morning. Since he was, they agreed to meet at Tim Horton's for a coffee.

"My! You're looking good, Gerry." Simon said as soon as they were seated.

"Sure thing, Simon! It's been an education for me to work at the Holiday Inn! I've observed how young guys dress and do their hair and my manager gives me tips he thinks will improve my image with the customers."

Simon took a good look at his long time friend while sipping his coffee and saw the difference more precisely. Whereas he used to live in faded blue jeans and a scruffy tee shirt he was now in a clean pair of chinos and a smart blue polo necked sweater. He also had his hair styled, rather than letting it grow long and untidy.

"Are you really happy working there or did I trap you in something you hate?" Simon said sincerely while peering into his eyes.

Gerry finished his mouthful of Danish and exclaimed, "Simon! You couldn't have done more for me! I'm going through training which will make me a manager, although I may have to transfer to get the promotion."

"I'm so glad but hope you won't be transferred too far away!"

"Oh, I'm ready for anything!" He finished drinking his coffee. "But how about you?"

"I'm on top of the world!" exclaimed Simon. "I've just moved in with Fran and said goodbye to the old homestead! I'm leasing a car and the job's good, so life is great!"

"I'm glad for you too!" Gerry mumbled and looked sad. "Wish I had a girl though!"

"It'll come Gerry! In your job you must see dozens of possibles!"

"I do but I'm still rather shy so I don't have a good approach!"

"Would you like me to help you?"

"Gee! If you would!" Gerry said more brightly. "What do you suggest?"

"How about we go right now to the Holiday Inn and inspect the merchandise!"

"Done!" They both left their chairs and went out to Simon's car, Gerry running his hands over the glossy body-work in silent admiration.

When they entered the Holiday Inn Gerry guided Simon to a staff rest room. It was sparsely furnished with a couple of chairs and a small table. Sitting on one of the chairs was a young woman of about twenty five holding a cup of coffee. She stared at them in surprise.

"Oh, it's you Gerry," she said, "I thought you were off today."

"I just popped in with my friend, Simon, to see what was going on."

She smiled at Simon and said, "Nice to meet you Simon. Would you like a coffee?"

"No thanks. I came with Gerry because he told me there were some nice people working here." He gave her a wide grin. "I can see what he means! You do look very nice!"

Gerry was blushing and seemed embarrassed at Simon's approach but he found the courage to say, "I've always thought you very nice, Val."

"It seems to me," said Simon, "that you two ought to get together on your off days! Gerry's been my friend since our college days and we've been the best of pals!"

Val laughed. "I suspect a plot! You've cooked this up together haven't you?"

"Not really, Val," Gerry said earnestly, "we were just passing!"

"Sure you were," she replied, "but I'm glad you did!" She put her coffee cup on the table and stood up. Simon noticed that she was an inch or two taller than Gerry but had a full figure similar to his friend. She was smartly dressed in navy blue pants and a cream sweater.

Gerry moved closer to her and asked timidly, "Would you like to go to the movies next time we're off together?"

"Thanks, Gerry. I'd like that!" She moved around him to leave the room and loudly whispered. "But don't bring Simon, will you?"

Simon laughed and thought the meeting augured well for his friend.

"She's on the desk, like me, but only does days. So we'll have to work together to find a time when we can meet."

"Never mind, Gerry, my old buck! She took the invite without hesitation. Now you've got to look at the duty schedules."

"Thanks for your help, again! Will you give me a ride home?"

After dropping Gerry off at his home, Simon drove to Francesca's place and was pleased to find her there. It was a beautiful afternoon and, having nothing better to do, he suggested they go out for a drive.

"Fran," he said tentatively, "would you like to go out to see Ahmid's place? I'm curious to see where he lives and what facilities he has?"

"Don't you think I see enough of that place when I go to work?"

"Yes, I know but I want to see whether he has any large storage barns on the property which might facilitate him packing drugs."

"Well, okay then. I'll come with you and it might be an education for you to see how hard it is for me to travel out there every day!"

Simon was surprised by her comment, as she had never mentioned the travel before. "Yes it would be a help in that way. Maybe we can find a solution?"

"Huh! Not with Grand River Transport you won't!"

He went over to hug her and said, "It doesn't have to be for ever!"

She kissed him as he released her and said, "Come on then! Let's get going!"

They grabbed jackets, got in the car, and made their way out of the City to St. Agatha.

It was a small township centred on the intersection of two significant roads which carried the only traffic light in the area. There was some scattered commercial development around this focus but the housing was sprinkled away from the intersection. Simon turned east from the road he had taken out of Waterloo and they passed old and new homes which became sparse after about half a kilometre. Francesca told him to slow.

"Ahmid's house is down the next side road on the right. You might miss it if you were going fast."

They turned left when the lane appeared and Simon drove slowly along it until Francesca told him to stop. They were alongside an old stone farmhouse set back from the lane.

"This is the place. I have to walk here from the traffic signals every day!"

Simon got out of the car and surveyed the property. Behind the house he could see at least two other wooden buildings; presumably barns when the place was an active farm. He could not see any human activity around the buildings but noticed the gravel driveway was well used. Then he joined Fran in the car again.

"What is the house like inside?" he asked.

"It's beautiful! It's all been modernized and furnished with expensive stuff, as far as I can tell."

"Where do you work in the house?"

"There's an office at the back which is used by Ahmid and he lets me work there on his records."

"Have you assimilated any ideas about his actual business process?"

"Well, yes! All I do is to check off the documents involving imports that come with an invoice for him to pay and link the items to dealers

who do the retail selling." She answered, looking at him with a puzzled glance.

"And you think it's all pretty straightforward, do you?"

"I don't know what you're expecting of me, Simon, but I can't see any mysteries in what he's doing."

Simon turned in his seat to face her squarely. "I know you think I'm strange, expecting you to find clues in his transactions just because I have this suspicion about where his income comes from. All I know is that from what I've learned on the Internet about income of entrepreneurs is that they don't make the kind of money our friend here does!"

"But are you comparing apples with apples? Do these other people deal in the same goods?"

"No, some do, some don't. It depends on the type of goods they import. That's why I think something else is going on."

Francesca sighed with exasperation. "I can't see what else there is in his business! Maybe you should drop the whole thing" She flung her open hands onto her knees. "It all happened because your darned sister found some powder in a box she bought. I don't see why you should get involved with such a slim issue!"

Simon could see she was getting angry. "Sorry, my love! I do poke my nose into things, don't I?" He gave her a peck on the cheek. "Just one other thing! Would you get me the names and addresses of his retailers? Then, I'll give it a rest unless something more substantial turns up."

"That's good! Can we go home now?"

"Sure!" Simon turned the car and accelerated down the lane.

CHAPTER FOURTEEN

On Friday of the following week, Francesca presented Simon with a list of retailers with whom Ahmid Singh was dealing. There were only six of them, most in the Toronto area, but there was one name that struck a cord with them. It was the Company who had a stall in the Market, from whom Samantha had bought her jewellery box, and was called "Far East Frivolities". The owner's name was Art Mesilla and he lived in Cambridge.

"Do you think you'd like to join me one night in exploring this Company's premises?" Simon asked Francesca.

"I'm sorry, Simon, but I don't want to get into any dangerous sleuthing! I really can't understand why you seem so obsessed with the idea that drugs are involved. If you must go on, why don't you try to get one of your gang to help. I know they said they were all busy but, with your charm, you could twist an arm and get one of them to help!"

"Okay, if that's how you feel about it, I'll give Vernon a call."

Vernon's name came to mind for Simon because he was in a very practical job. As a trainee Heating and Cooling Engineer it seemed reasonable to assume he'd be able to manipulate locks to open doors or see weak entry points to a building. Simon picked up the phone and dialled Vernon's home number that he retrieved from his diary. After two rings a female voice answered.

"Could I speak with Vernon?" Simon asked.

"You could if he was here!" the sprightly voice replied. "He's out on a job this evening. You could try his Cell!"

"Thanks. What's the number?"

He jotted it down as the woman recited it and then dialled.

"Hello" said Vernon.

"Hi, there, buddy! It's Simon! Are you busy?"

"Oh! How're yer doin'? I haven't missed one of our wing nights, have I?"

Simon laughed. "NO, nothing that disastrous! Are you up for a bit of breaking and entering?"

"Is it legal? Or is it chancy?"

"The latter, I'm afraid, but we don't want to steal anything. Just a look around!"

"Well, see here, Simon. I've got another half hour to finish this job then I can meet you and you can tell me what this is all about. Okay?"

"Thanks, Vernon. You're a sport! The place I'd like to see is in Cambridge. How about we meet in the Mall by MacDonald's in an hour?"

"That's fine. I'm already in Cambridge. I'll see you there!"

Simon told Francesca of this arrangement and went to put on some black clothing and rubber-soled pumps.

When he came down again from his room she laughed. "You look a right sleuth in that gear! The police could arrest you with intent before you begin!"

"I don't think so! I don't look that suspicious! I'm only going to meet Vernon!"

"Well, my love, just be careful. I need you back here!"

They exchanged a kiss and Simon went out to his car.

Simon did not have long to wait in the Mall before Vernon arrived in his typical work clothes of blue jeans and grey sweater. They greeted one another with a quick hug and decided to buy a coffee so that Simon could explain what he needed. When Vernon heard the story of possible drugs in a wooden jewellery box, he leaned away from Simon and threw his hands in the air.

"Hold it, brother! This sounds much too risky with drugs being involved."

"No, it's just a brief incursion to see what activities go on in this man's place. I don't expect to find a big grow-op or a cocaine hoard. I'd just like to examine wooden boxes to see if they're empty."

"Where will that get you?" Vernon asked.

"I shall be able to decide whether the boxes are imported with drugs already in them or whether this guy fills them here."

"Then what?"

"I could go to the police and leave it to them to take some action."

Vernon looked pensive and shrugged his shoulders. "I don't understand why you're getting involved at all, Simon. But, I'll tell you what I'll do for our friendship's sake! I'll come to this place you've got an address for and, if it's commercial, I'll help you get in. Then I leave! Okay?"

"You're a real decent guy" declared Simon. "I can't expect more help than that!"

They both stood up and made their way to their cars. Simon led the way to the address he had already planned out. He stopped outside a large metal warehouse building with wide doors facing the road and big enough to admit a truck. The two men met together in front of the doors. Vernon appraised them and attempted to slide them to one side. There was little movement.

"I don't see how we can get in through these doors," Vernon announced.

"Maybe, there's some other entry round the back?" suggested Simon.

He started walking down one side of the building. It was very dark because the adjacent warehouse was close enough to screen any light from the street lamps. Simon walked the full depth of the building and part way round the back. On returning to his friend he said, "There's a small door in the back. Looks like it has a Yale lock."

Without speaking Vernon walked to the back and stopped in front of a regular house door. "If I can open the lock here, Simon, I'll do it and then go. Okay?"

"That's fine. Don't you go inside, then you won't be accused of entering, only breaking!"

They both laughed and Vernon took out a bunch of keys from his pocket. He fiddled for some time before one key finally turned the lock. He opened the door. "There you are, my friend. This is as far as I go!"

"Thanks, Vernon. You're a wonder! See you soon!" said Simon as he entered the building.

Once inside, he closed the door and tried to take stock of his surroundings with the aid of a small pocket torch he had brought. To one side there was a wooden desk with a telephone on it. Next to it was a standard four drawer metal filing cabinet. Simon pulled on one of the drawer handles and it opened. Inside there were only remnants of a lunch and a half-empty coffee cup. He quickly skimmed through all the drawers and only the top one had actual files in hanging folders. Upon examination he discovered that each file was devoted to letters and invoices for a particular merchant. He assumed these to be people who were also selling the imported goods. It might be useful information, he decided, but he wanted to examine the actual goods, which he believed to be in the warehouse he'd broken into. Moving his torch around he saw another door and found it opened into a large black cavernous space. He walked in.

Never had he felt such a sense of fear overcome him. The place was in total darkness and carried a strange acrid smell like smouldering vegetation. He went to switch on his torch but fumbled with it and it fell with a soft rustling sound. Again he felt that strange prickling sensation of the unknown and bent down to pick up his torch. He had to move his hand around to try and locate it and, as he did so, he felt both dry and wet material on the floor. Some of it felt slimy and made him shudder. The dry stuff rustled as his hand moved through it to search for his torch and it seemed as if some creature was actually crawling over his hand. He involuntarily moved his whole arm back and up and felt particles of the unknown material spatter his face. Again he bent over to try to locate his torch and, as he did so, an intensely bright light blinded him. An unusual voice shouted, "Stay where you are! I've a gun on you!"

Simon straightened himself and tried to see beyond the light. No matter how he twisted his head around he could make out nothing until the other being lowered the beam and drew nearer.

"Who are you?" He involuntarily blurted out.

"More to the point, who are you!" the stranger replied as he moved closer.

Simon could see he was holding a revolver and wore some kind of uniform clothing.

"Well," Simon began searching his brain for an excuse, "I was looking for a place to kip for the night and your back door was open, so I came in."

"I don't believe you!" Said the other man in a gruff voice. "You had a torch before you dropped it. Street people don't usually carry torches." He turned his lantern to point at the ground and commanded, "Come here!"

"Put your gun away and I will," Simon replied.

The man did as he was asked and Simon took a few paces nearer. His opponent was taller than himself by several inches. He had a swarthy face of far eastern hue and seemed to be about three hundred pounds in weight. Simon mentally dismissed any idea of making a break. Instead he asked, "What are you gong to do with me?"

"Take you to my boss!" He waved his lantern to indicate a direction. "This way! Get moving!"

Simon ambled forward in the direction indicated. From the general light of the lantern he saw they were moving through a large building with growing plants on one side and boxes stacked on the other. He would have liked to get into the boxes and prove his theory but he received regular prods in his back to keep him moving. Suddenly he halted and pointed to the plants.

"What on earth are you growing here?" he asked.

A more vigorous prod moved him on again and his captor did not reply. They finally reached a door that was the opposite end of the building from the one in which Simon had entered. The man pushed him aside and opened the door with a key. It was still dark but the street lights helped Simon to orient himself. Nearby an SUV vehicle was parked and he noticed his own car was still across the road where he'd left it. "Get in," the man said with a shove towards the passenger door of the vehicle.

"Where're you taking me?" asked Simon as he opened the door and sat in the SUV.

The man got into his driver's seat and started the motor. "You'll know when we get there!" he said.

They drove for an hour and Simon knew they were leaving the City. Buildings along the way became sparse and eventually there was nothing but countryside bathed under a fading moon. Finally, they turned into a gravelled drive which led to a farmhouse.

The driver alighted and came round to Simon's side. Keeping him covered with his gun, he indicated that Simon should get out and go to the door of the building. It was a well-weathered oak door with wrought iron handle and latch. The big man clicked on the latch and put his shoulder to the door. It opened into a completely black hallway. Simon was pushed inside unceremoniously and fell to the paved floor. Before he could raise himself he was aware of a light in the distance which slowly came closer. He finally pushed himself up and looked to see who was carrying the light. He was totally stunned when he recognized the person as Ahmid Singh.

It was not he, alone who was stunned, for Ahmid took a pace back and gasped, "What are you doing here, Simon?"

"I-I-I don't know!" he stuttered in reply. "I was brought here by that guy behind me." He turned to look at his captor to be sure he was still there. It was all seeming to be like a nightmare.

The captor spoke up. "I found this fellow in your warehouse, sir. I don't know how he got in because there was no evidence of forced entry. I guess he used a key to open our back door?"

"Did you get into my warehouse, Simon? And why?" asked Ahmid.

"It's a long story, sir. Do you think we could sit down 'cause I'm rather tired!"

"Of course!" Ahmid displayed no sense of annoyance or anger at Simon's intrusion. "Come into the back where I have a little sitting room."

They all followed Ahmid with his torch to the rear of the building and into a cosy room with a fire burning in the hearth. There were just three chairs so each man took his position facing into a circle.

"Now, what's this all about?" asked Ahmid in his usual precise manner of talking.

Simon took a deep breath and began. "I have to admit, first of all Mister Singh, that I became suspicious of the large deposits you were making in Henry Allbine's investments."

Ahmid nodded his head in understanding.

"Next," Simon continued, "my sister bought a wooden box in which she discovered some white powder. She works in a Hospital and had the powder analyzed by the laboratory manager who said it was cocaine or some similar drug. I'm afraid I then jumped to the conclusion that you could have been importing dugs illegally by hiding them in those boxes and that's how you made such a lot of money."

Both of the other two laughed in unison as if they had heard a great joke. Ahmid said, "Oh, Simon, you have been reading too many cheap novels and your mind has been warped.! Your girl friend works for me now. Surely she could tell you from her knowledge of my records that my income is entirely from the sale of my imports?"

He sat back and smiled at the young interloper with fatherly indulgence. Then his voice became stern. "However, Simon, we cannot have you poking around in our store. I'm afraid we must keep you hidden for a while."

"You can't do that!" Declared Simon. "There'll be no end of people wanting to know where I've got to, including the Police."

"Well, I don't want to harm you but we need a little time to clear our warehouse, after which we can release you and no harm will be done." Ahmid turned to his assistant and said, "Jacob, lock him up in the basement. Give him some food and drink and blankets. He should be safe for a while."

The big captor stood and grabbed Simon's arm. He was propelled down some rough stairs to a cold basement where he was flung into a room with a heavy door that the man secured with a bolt on the outside.

CHAPTER FIFTEEN

Although Francesca went to bed the same evening that Simon had left, she could not sleep. Several times during the night and early morning she went downstairs to see whether he had returned, intermittently making herself a warm drink. Finally, at five thirty, she got dressed and phoned the police. Her short conversation with the desk sergeant only confirmed what she expected from them. *Sorry, madam he's an adult and only missing less that twenty-four hours, so we can't institute a search yet.*

She thought back on what he'd said last night. He was dressed in black and she'd said he looked like a burglar but he said he was only going to meet Vernon. This was one of the pals he'd met at a pub night not long ago. Maybe she could phone him? She went up to Simon's room to look for his diary. Luckily, he hadn't taken it with him, so she looked up Vernon's number and dialled.

"Could I speak to Vernon, please?"

"Well, I don't know as he's awake yet! You're calling pretty early. Is it urgent? Who are you, anyway?"

Francesca hadn't realized it was still only shortly after six but she persisted and said hurriedly. "Sorry about the time but I think he went out with Simon last night. I'm Francesca! Has he returned?"

"'Course 'e has. Didn't I say 'e was asleep?"

"Yes. I'm sorry! Simon hasn't come home and I'm worried."

"Oh, lor, deary! You must be worried?" The cheery voice at the other end of the line became serious. "Look, I'm Missus Spreitzer, Vernon's wife. Let me call 'im and get 'im to call you back. Okay?"

"Thank you very much," said Francesca. "What's your name, by the way?"

"I'm Angela! Maybe we'll meet some day? I'll hang up now and get Vern to call you."

As Francesca put the phone down she thought it strange that Vernon's wife would be up while he still slept. Her attitude with Simon was to wait getting up herself until he was clear of the bathroom. Hardly had this thought passed through her head when the phone rang and she grabbed it.

"Hello! Is this Vernon?"

"Yes. You must be a very worried woman! You say Simon hasn't returned home?"

"That's right. I did call the police but they can't help. What happed to you both last night? Simon looked as if he was ready to burgle some place."

"You're right, Fran! I opened a door for Simon and saw him go in, then I left for home. Wonder what's happened to him?"

"Oh, I wish I could find out!" groaned Francesca. "I don't know what else to do."

"Well, it is still early. Any chance he might have got himself a breakfast and then went in to work?"

"That's an idea." replied Francesca. "I could call his office."

"You do that, dearie! Hope you soon hear from him."

She phoned the office of Henry Allbine but only got an answering machine to say they were open at nine. She paced the room and chewed on her finger nails.. At eight thirty she called the home of Ahmid Singh to let him know she would be late arriving for work.

He answered the phone himself and said, "Thank you for letting me know, Francesca. Take your time getting here. There's no hurry!"

"Thank you, Mister Singh!" As she hung up, she wondered why he hadn't asked what was causing the delay but dismissed it quickly because the phone rang again.

"This is Henry Allbine, here. Simon hasn't reported in for work yet. Is he okay?"

"I don't know, Mister Allbine. He hasn't been home all night." She felt the tears pooling in her eyes and feared she would burst out crying. "I'm so worried! It's not like him to go away and not tell me."

"Well, don't worry! Perhaps he had an urgent call from his family?"

"Yes, I suppose that's possible."

"Have you called them?"

"Well, no, I haven't. Maybe I should do that now."

"Yes. You do that and let me know."

She went to Simon's room again to get his diary. After finding the number for his parents' home, she dialled. A woman answered with a mature voice and she assumed it was his mother.

"Is that Missus Lightward? This is Francesca, Simon's girl friend."

"How nice of you to call me, my dear. I don't think we've met but I hope we shall soon."

"You sound like a very friendly person but I must ask for your help. Simon has disappeared."

"Good heavens," Simon's Mother declared, "How long has he been away?"

"Actually, it's only since yesterday evening. He was away all night. I've told the police and his employer, Mister Allbine has called me. It was he who suggested I phone you."

"I'm so glad you did. You must be very worried. Do you want to come over here and tell me all about it?"

"You're so kind! I'd like to do that." Francesca answered feeling thankful that somebody cared. "When shall I come?"

"Well, now, dear child! We can have a coffee together!"

Francesca had to catch a bus to get to the Lightward's house so it was about forty minutes before she arrived. Missus Lightward opened the door quickly when she knocked and immediately gave her a healthy hug.

"Come on in, my dear! It's Francesca, isn't it? I'm Joan, look you! Do they call you Fran?"

Francesca stepped inside and was led into the living room. She felt warm and secure by the welcome and gratefully sank into an armchair.

"Will you have some coffee?" asked Joan. "I have a fresh pot all ready. How do you take it?"

"Cream and one sugar, thank you!" Francesca relaxed more completely. She felt more secure than she'd ever known while living with her Aunt. While waiting for the coffee, she looked around at the richness and warmth of the room. She felt she could understand where Simon was coming from and it pleased her.

"Here we are," said Joan as she placed a cup from the tray she carried onto the side table and then settled herself into another arm chair. "I've never enjoyed a woman to woman chat like this for ages!"

Fran laughed, feeling so much at ease. "And this is so helpful in relieving my anxiety."

They sipped coffee for a while before Joan said, "So, tell me! How did my Simon come to disappear?"

Fran related as much as she knew about the drug powder, Simon's assumption about Mister Singh's wealth, and his desire to check out the warehouse where stuff may be stored. She explained that she'd talked to Vernon who had gone with Simon to a building in Cambridge and learned that he only opened the door and then went home, leaving Simon to investigate on his own.

"MY! It does seem rash of Simon to do this but he never did leave problems unsolved in his mind. Could he have been captured by the security guards at this warehouse, do you think?" Joan asked in almost a single breath.

"I suppose that could be so but what can we do to find him?" asked Fran.

There was a long silence before Joan spoke again. "I really don't know, my dear. I can only suggest you be patient and, if he doesn't return within two days, tell the Police again."

"Hmm! I don't think I can just do nothing. I think I'll go to Ahmid Singh, who employs me on a part time basis, and get him to show me this warehouse which must be owned by a retailer to whom he sells his imports."

"That sounds like a good idea! But, please be careful! You don't know that mister Singh is not in league with his retailers, do you?"

"You've been so kind to me, I hope I'll see you again." Francesca stood up. "I feel I must go now and catch a bus to Mister Singh's home. I've already told him I'll be late and now, I'm later still!"

Joan Lightward escorted her guest to the door and they exchanged hugs and kisses.

When Francesca arrived at the Singh home she rehearsed in her head just what she would say to Mister Singh. He opened the door to her knock and greeted her with a smile and a brief, "So there you are!" and stepped back into the hall to allow her to walk in.

"I'm very sorry to be so late, Mister Singh, but I phoned Simon's Mother and she invited me to coffee, so I was glad of her sympathy. I hope you can forgive me?"

"Please don't be concerned about being late to my place. Where I come from, people are often late for appointments!" He remarked in a jovial voice. "But come into the office!"

Together they made their way to the back of the house where Ahmid Singh had his office, which was also his den. There were several books and vouchers set out in an orderly fashion on the desk.

"Is there anything in particular you'd like me to do now I'm here, or shall I just go through my usual routine?" asked Francesca.

"Before you do that, I wish you'd tell me what caused your anxiety this morning. Is there anything I can do?"

Francesca felt relieved that he invited her to tell him about her worries so she started, "Simon didn't come home last night---- you do know he lives with me now, don't you?"

Ahmid's thick eyebrows lifted at once. "No, young lady, I did not know that!"

"Well, he does, and I was worried when he didn't return after a meeting he had with a friend. It's not like him to keep me in the dark about his affairs but he went out to his meeting dressed like a burglar."

Ahmid began to feel anxious because he was holding Simon prisoner and could not afford to tell Francesca at this time. "What have you done, so far, to try to locate him?"

"I called the police at first but they can do nothing this early. Then I called his friend who knew where they went but left before Simon went into the building. Finally, I told Simon's Mother. She was very sympathetic but could suggest anything to help. So now I guess I'm in your hands?"

Mister Singh was at a loss to know what to say. "Well, this is-er-very unusual. It is still very early in his disappearance. I can only urge you to be patient. I'm sure you'll hear from him within the next day or two!"

"Thank you, sir! You are very kind. Shouldn't I get on with my work?"

"Of course! Do what ever you feel you can manage! I must leave you to attend to my business." He got up and left her alone.

He immediately went to another phone to call his assistant. "Jacob! Have you still got our nosy intruder locked up?"

"Of course! I took him breakfast this morning."

"That's good," Ahmid assured him. "I've had his girl friend here and she is worried. I would not like to detain him longer than is necessary."

"I think we could have the warehouse empty in two days from now."

"That is excellent. Keep up the good work, Jacob!"

CHAPTER SIXTEEN

Francesca's return home that evening was miserable. She'd had no hope of finding Simon in spite of the many contacts she'd made. The house was cold and uninviting with mail scattered over the hall floor which was sure evidence that Simon had not returned. She felt like crying like never before; even when her Aunt had died and she was alone. Bending down to pick up the mail, she noticed a coating of dust over the wood block floor and was reminded that she hadn't done any general cleaning for at least a month. Somehow, that changed her spirits. "I'll clean up tonight so it's all attractive for when Simon comes home!" She said aloud and hastened into the kitchen to make a bit of supper. There was a piece of frozen salmon in the freezer which she cooked in the microwave and the remains of a pasta salad she'd made yesterday. "That'll do me before I get down to my clean up." She switched on the radio to a local channel and was embraced by a comforting melody.

Sometime after nine o'clock, as she was putting away her vacuum cleaner, the phone rang. Dropping the cleaner hose she quickly lifted the handset. "Hello!" she said.

"Is that Fran? This is Vern, here!"

"Oh! Good to hear from you!" she responded, wondering whether he had news. "Have you heard from Simon or know anything about him?"

"Sorry, dear, but no! --Well, not directly! I was wondering about his car. Did you pick it up?"

"No-o-o! I don't drive, so it never gave me a thought. In any case I don't know where Simon left it."

"Of course, I know where he left it last night,so I thought I'd go and see if it's still there."

"Would you, Vern? If it's there, you could bring it home."

"Well, you say you don't drive, otherwise I was going to suggest that you come with me to drive it back. Now, I suppose, I'd better try one of our gang to see if someone can come with me."

"Oh, if you would, Vern. I'd be so grateful!" She was thinking that it could be some comfort to at least see Simon's car in the drive again.

"Alright, Fran. I'll see whether I can get one of the guys to come with me." He paused. "You do realize I've got no key and the car may not be there, still?"

"Let me slip up to his room and see if I can find the spare." She hurried up to Simon's room and went to the drawer where he kept his diary. Sure enough, it lay among bills and bank statements. She ran down to the phone again. "Yes I've got the spare! Will you come round and get it now?"

"Okay! Give me about half hour to try to bring one of the others with me? See yer later."

Francesca paced around with impatience while waiting for Vernon to return. It seemed to her that the recovery of Simon's car would automatically bring his return closer but she knew it was an absurd notion. She cursed herself for being too idle to take some driving lessons while she had the chance. After all, her Aunt had a car and she could have got her to give some instruction but it was too late now as she'd sold the car soon after her aunt was buried. At last, there was a ring at the door and she hurried to open it. Vern stood there with a shorter fatter young fellow whose name she couldn't remember.

"Come in," she said, "and I'll give you the key."

"No! We can't stay as Gerry here is really at work so we've got to do this in a rush!"

Now she remembered. Gerry worked at the Holiday Inn. "I'll get the key for you!"

She retrieved it from the kitchen table and returned to the front door to hand it to Vernon. "You'll take care of it, won't you?" she said needlessly.

He turned without saying any more and the two of them hurried out to his car.

When they reached the location of the warehouse that Vernon had broken into the previous night, he was amazed to see Simon's car still on the gravel verge where he'd parked it. He and Gerry inspected the vehicle carefully to make sure the wheel hubs had not been stolen or the inside of the car ransacked. They remarked that Simon was lucky he hadn't left it in New York!

Gerry got in and familiarized himself with the control arrangement while Vernon went to his own vehicle. Once Gerry had started the motor and turned on the lights, Vernon drove off and they proceeded in tandem to Francesca's home. There, Gerry parked in her gravel drive and gave her the key. He rushed off back to Vernon to get a ride to resume his Hotel duties. They had a laugh together when Gerry said, "Simon would tell us, 'It's not quite form, y'know! Taking all this time off!' in the precise way he always talks of matters of ethics!"

Francesca, meanwhile, couldn't resist the temptation to sit in Simon's car in an attempt to inhale the feeling of his physical presence to comfort her in some slight way for the coming restless night.

*   *   *   *

Simon had been imprisoned for two nights and was getting very bored. He'd inspected his cell closely to see whether he could find a weak spot to work on for an escape. The whole place was built of stone; more like hard granite than sandstone; so he knew he had little chance of burrowing out somehow. There was no window, the only light coming from a bare bulb hanging from the ceiling, and they had taken everything from his pockets except a ball-point pen.

His captor, Jacob, brought him regular meals which were always hot and very palatable. He'd tried to engage him in conversation but

Jacob remained uncommunicative. However he did bring in a couple of books which helped Simon relieve the monotony even though they were very old Victorian tales of the Charles Dickens style and full of black and white sketches.

Now, on this third morning he made up his mind to trick Jacob and, if he was quick enough, to run out the door and bolt it. Since Jacob spoke very little he wondered what he could do to attract his attention in some way. He used his pen to do some shading on the illustrations of the book in the hope that he could draw Jacob's attention away from the door so that he could slip behind him. He knew it was no use trying to knock the man unconscious in view of his size and strength; his only asset was speed.

Jacob came in with lunch and set it on the end of the bed as usual. Simon was sitting at the head of the bed, farthest away from the door, and with back to it, pretended to be immersed in one of the books. He did not speak and continued shading a picture with his pen. Jacob moved nearer and peered over Simon's shoulder.

"Found yerself somefink to do, 'ave yer?"

Simon shot upright and thrust the book at Jacob whose instinctive reaction was to take it.

"Yes! Have a good look at my drawings!" He said as he backed toward the door.

"What fer?" asked Jacob looking intently at the book he held.

"Keep looking," cried Simon as, with a lightening move, he slipped out the door. He just had time to slam it shut and push the bolt on the outside home when he heard Jacob hammer on it and shout something threatening.

Simon waited no longer. He shot up the stone stairs and into the main hall of the house. Would he find the front door unlocked, he wondered? When he reached it, how relieved he felt to see it was a Yale lock with a knob on the inside to open it. He could no longer hear any shouts from the basement and guessed Jacob was alone in the place since no one else appeared. He at once headed for the driveway which took him to a paved highway and he ran along it as fast as he knew how, continually looking back over his shoulder to see if he was being followed. After a few hundred metres of running he paused to regain his breath. The highway had been quite deserted of traffic until that moment but now he spied a Mennonite horse and buggy with only one driver. He stepped into the road and waved his hands. The driver pulled the horse to a stop.

"What's the trouble, young feller?" asked the driver in a gentle tone of voice.

"Could you give me a ride to wherever you're going? I need to get a bus to take me to Waterloo."

"Sure! Hop up alongside me!" The driver moved over to make room on the wooden seat under the covered awning and Simon climbed aboard. Without delay, the man flicked the reins and the buggy rolled smoothly forward. Simon gave a sigh of relief. He was conscious of the smell of the horse and leather which he found comforting and natural. He thought that if they did see anyone from the farmhouse where he'd been held captive, they might ignore this vehicle with its sombre black clad driver, so he hunkered down as low as he could.

"It's not usual to see a person walking on this road in the afternoon," said the driver, "have you got lost?"

"Well, in a way, you could say I was lost but I want to get home as soon as possible."

"I'm going into St Agatha for some stores. I can drop you there and you can wait for a bus or hitch another ride."

"That would be perfect, thank you. I have no money on me so can't offer to give you anything by way of thanks."

The driver laughed and explained, "We don't accept gifts when we help out our fellow man! We do it as an act of our beliefs."

"I see! You're most kind and you have helped me more than you'll ever know."

They were entering the Township and more traffic passed them. Simon noticed a few people loitering on the sidewalks and knew he must be careful not to show himself if he could avoid it. When the driver pulled the horse to a stop, Simon climbed down and shook his hand. "Thank you again." he said as he hurried away to hide in a shop doorway. He listened to the clip-clop of the horse's hooves fading into the distance before he emerged and tried to locate a bus stop near the cross roads in the Township. It was well identified and he looked at a tattered timetable attached to a post. If the information was still valid, he should have no more than ten minutes to wait.

At that point, however, he realized again that he had no money or ID to pay his fare. He had to find a phone and call Francesca. He just hoped she was not at work today. Keeping his eye out for possible strangers who might be following him, he made his way to a filling station where he expected to find a phone. Sure enough they had one and the person on duty allowed him to use it to call Waterloo. He dialled Fran's number and waited in tense anticipation to hear her voice.

"Hello!" she said and Simon let out a sigh of relief.

"Thank God!" he exclaimed. "It's Simon here, darling, I'm in St Agatha! Have you got the car? Could you come and get me?"

"Oh, sweetheart!" she replied, tears almost welling out of her eyes, "I thought I might never see you again. How do you come to be in St Agatha?"

He laughed. "That's a very long story! Right now I want to get away from here as quickly as possible. Can you help me? I've no money or credit cards."

"Well, darling, Vernon and Gerry got your car back here but I can't drive! What would you like me to do?"

"I can't wait while you try to get one of our gang to drive; I might be seen. Will you call a cab and come up to fetch me?"

"Why can't you get a cab in the Township and I will pay when he gets here?"

"Hold on a tick! I'll ask the assistant here if there is a cab."

He turned to the attendant who had just finished serving a customer. "Can I get a cab to take me to Waterloo?"

"You can, but that customer is just going there. I'll give him a shout to see if he'll take you." He ran over to the car and spoke with the driver. "Yes. He'll give you a ride."

Simon spoke in the phone again and told Francesca what had been arranged and then entered the waiting vehicle.

"It's very kind of you to take me," he said, settling himself in the passenger seat. "I've lost my money and need to get home."

"No problem!" the driver explained patiently. "I have to go into Waterloo to make some calls so I'll drop you off somewhere convenient."

They moved off and in twenty minutes were entering the Town. Simon asked to be dropped in the Town Centre and then walked about a kilometre to Francesca's place. When she opened the door to his knock she screamed with delight and dragged him inside. They hugged and kissed and she said, "Simon, I've never been as worried as I've been over the last three days! I love you so much! Please don't do anything risky again!"

"And I've come to realize how much I love you, dearest. I don't want to be separated again!"

"Come and sit down, then, and tell me all about it."

*   *   *   *

Ahmid Singh was on his way to pay his evening visit to his farmhouse, located about half an hour's drive west of St Agatha. He had bought it to provide a quiet building to process the various products that came his way. Some came in from his brother in Pakistan and some came from the man who rented the Waterloo warehouse from him. He only employed Jacob directly in this business because he planned to keep himself well removed from the direct production of the special health drug alternatives he marketed. Jacob owed him allegiance because he had saved his life in India before coming to Canada.

When he got to the farmhouse he was surprised to find the front door open. He made a lot of noise banging on the door and shouting for Jacob. Total silence was the only response. Cautiously he stepped into the hall and advanced to the stairs to the basement. He called out Jacob's name and then heard a hammering on the cellar door.

"Who's there?" he shouted.

"It's Jacob! Let me out!"

Ahmid withdrew the bolt and the door burst open. A dishevelled and tired looking Jacob fell into his employer's arms.

"My dear fellow," said an astonished Ahmid. "What has happened?"

"Very sorry, sir. I was tricked and Simon escaped."

"Did he hurt you? How did he trick you?'

"He was busy drawing in a book when I took 'im 'is lunch I was a stupid fool 'cos I went to 'ave a gander at wot he was doing. He skipped be'ind me back an' shut the door on me. It's all my fault, sir. I 'ope I 'aven't corsed you touble?"

What time did he get away?" asked Ahmid.

"Abart two o'clock I fink."

"Hmm! He will be clear by now but I've been told the Warehouse is empty, so he's no evidence to give to the police. Don't worry, my friend. Anyone could have reacted as you did, as long as you told him nothing?"

"No, sir, I was very careful not to speak to 'im."

"That is good, Jacob. It is not that I am involved in anything criminal you understand. It is just that I want to protect my products from imitation."

"I know that, sir, and I've been packing boxes of your jars just like you told me. There's a lot to send out."

"Thank you, Jacob. I will arrange to collect them tomorrow."

CHAPTER SEVENTEEN

Simon and Francesca spent a long time sharing their experiences of the last three days. They slept together and made love; each telling of how their growing feelings toward the other had developed while they were parted. When they awoke and had some breakfast Simon said, "I really should call Henry and tell him I'm on my way to the office."

"Must you, darling? I know you must call him but don't say when you'll come in."

"But it'll be dreadfully bad form not to go to work! He could well learn that I'm home! I'd like to stay with you but I feel the urge to do the right thing," pleaded Simon.

Francesca struck a disappointed face, jutting out her lower lip, "Oh, I suppose you *must* but I'm not going to the Singh's. I should probably tell Ahmid that I can't work for him again."

"Yes, because of me, you're in a difficult position. For now just say you won't be in."

"Okay! You call Henry, then!"

Simon took the phone and dialled. She heard him say "it's Simon here!" and then there was silence while Simon listened. Eventually he put the phone down and said, "Guess what? He doesn't want me in until tomorrow!"

"Isn't that great!" exclaimed Francesca. "What shall we do?"

"How about going back to bed?"

She giggled. "It'd be nice but I think I should report to the police that you're safe."

"Alright, spoil sport! Shall we go round to the station?"

"Why not? It's only five minutes drive."

Without saying any more they left and, after picking up a Tim Horton's coffee at the drive through, they reached the local police station.

They walked up to the counter and Francesca said to the Sergeant who acknowledged her, "A few days ago I reported my friend missing. You couldn't do anything at that time because he was an adult and had only been away 24 hours. Well, he's back now. I thought you should know!"

The serious faced officer behind the desk had listened intently to what Francesca had said and asked, "When did you report this, madam, and what is your name?" He reached under the counter and produced a large book.

"It was three days ago I made the report and I'm Francesca Mourie."

He flicked through a few pages and said, "Yes, madam, it was noted in the journal." He looked up at her and asked, "So what is the situation now?"

Simon couldn't restrain himself, "Well, I'm back, is all!"

The Officer turned his sombre gaze on Simon. "And you are?"

"Simon Lightward!"

"Are you related to Ms Mourie?"

Simon smiled broadly. "Not yet but I shall be soon!"

The officer turned to Francesca. "Is this gentleman the one you reported missing?"

"That's right. He was kidnapped!"

"Oh! You didn't say that in the original report, did you?"

"Well, of course not. I didn't know then, did I?" Replied Francesca with a feeling of exasperation.

"Mister Lightward" The officer turned to Simon. "I must ask you to give a report about your kidnapping. It is a criminal offence, y'know."

"Oh, must I? I do so hate forms!"

"I must insist, sir. Just hang on a minute and I'll get an officer to assist you." He picked up the desk phone.

Simon groaned and whispered to Fran, " You shouldn't have told him that." Then he turned to face her and said, "Look, I'm really sorry I started all this nonsense about Ahmid and his drugs. I've caused a lot of trouble for everybody."

Francesca shrugged and moved away from the counter to allow another young woman to speak to the Officer. She seemed very agitated although she was smartly dressed.

"I've just had my purse stolen," she declared in a loud voice.

At that moment another police officer who appeared from a different office, asked Simon and Francesca to accompany him, so they heard no more of that report.

Seated at the table, the young officer set out a number of forms and smiled at them encouragingly. He took them through a number of questions before ever writing down their answers.

"So you reported the kidnapping, Miss Mourie?"

"No, I reported Simon being missing."

"So, Mister Lightward, you reported the kidnapping?"

"No!" replied Simon. "I was not in a position to do that because I was captive at the time!"

"I see! So when did you report the kidnapping?"

"This morning when I came to the station with Miss Mourie. Well, to be strictly accurate, she reported it!"

The young officer smiled encouragingly at Francesca. "So, you reported the kidnapping this morning? Why did you do that?"

Francesca heaved a deep sigh of exasperation. "I only reported that my friend was no longer missing. I felt it necessary to do that so that you wouldn't start looking for him!"

"I see!" said the officer, clearly not understanding the situation. "Then why are you reporting a kidnapping now?"

"Because that's why Simon was missing for three days. I thought it would explain things!"

Their young interrogator sat back in his chair and looked at the forms in front of him.

"If you'd prefer," Simon interceded, "we won't report a kidnapping? Maybe that would save a lot of forms?"

"I'm not sure," replied the officer. "I think I must ask my Sergeant." He stood up and left the room.

"You see what a pickle you've got us into?" asked Simon sharply."

"Yes, I'm sorry, Simon! I didn't think!"

"Well, never mind, now. If we can suggest we were mistaken about a kidnapping, perhaps we can leave."

Their hopes were shattered when the original interrogator returned with a tall, heavily built, police sergeant. The men drew chairs up to the table and the young policeman said, "This is Sergeant Williams. He will conduct the interview from now on."

Sergeant Williams turned piercing eyes on Simon. "Now, sir, please tell me. Were you kidnapped or not? Just answer 'Yes' or 'No'?"

"Yes," answered Simon very clearly. "I was kidnapped."

"Do you know who your kidnappers were?"

Simon hesitated. He had been treated gently by Jacob and Ahmid but felt it was necessary to tell the truth and reveal who they were. He explained briefly what had happened in the warehouse and who had been involved.

"Thank you, sir. You've made things very clear. When you've put all that on this form," he pushed a letter-sized document toward him, "we shall be in a position to apprehend the culprits."

"Must I really," asked Simon. "I find that forms don't do much to move the process along. Can't you get on with the apprehension business and call on me for any details you need?"

The Sergeant shook his head. "That's not the way we do it, sir. Please complete that form."

Simon looked at Francesca questioningly and he could see by her expression she wanted him to comply. "Very good, Sergeant. I'll do as you say!"

Some half hour later, they left the police station but Simon felt very dissatisfied. He had wanted to do some investigating himself to satisfy his suspicions about Ahmid's drug activities and now it was taken out of his hands. Although, since his captivity, he was no longer sure that Ahmid was involved in drug smuggling.

When they got indoors, Simon said, "I'm going to call a meeting of my friends and get their help to settle the question of Ahmid's suspicious activities."

"Simon, you're mad! Why don't you let the police do what they have to? Why expose yourself to possible risk?"

"It's my sister got me into this by having that white powder in her wooden jewel box analysed by the Hospital lab. I feel obliged to help her."

"Then why don't you tell her what's happened to you and see if she's still interested in doing anything about it?"

"Fair comment, darling! I'll call her tonight!"

*   *   *   *

In Ahmid Singh's farmhouse, Jacob was completing the packing of dozens of jars of his Boss's patent medicine. He knew it was good stuff because he'd used it himself to rub on aching muscles and had got quick relief, so he was careful to put one jar in each of the specially designed compartments so they should not be broken in transit. When all the boxes were full he labelled each one with a name and address that he got from a book and was impressed with the geographical distribution his Boss had achieved. He was proud to support this man who had saved him from death in India some fifteen years ago.

Now he went to the telephone and told Ahmid that all the boxes he had in the farmhouse were complete and ready for despatch.

"That's very good work, Jacob,`` Mr Singh praised him and then instructed him to wait for the truck and then return to Ahmid's home in order to assist his wife. He did not like that work because it was messy and involved crushing ripe pepper plants to extract the juice that was the important item in the cream. It made him sneeze all the time and Missus Singh was not very sympathetic to his discomfort since she did not have the same reaction. But he had learned to be patient, so he settled down to await the truck.

CHAPTER EIGHTEEN

Simon went back to work the next day. Henry Allbine welcomed him like a long lost son. They spent an hour together, during which time, Simon told his story of capture and confinement and Henry outlined major developments in his business. He became very alarmed that his assistant had taken such extreme action to try to prove Ahmid was trafficking in drugs and concerned to learn that Ahmid Singh had been involved in Simon's kidnapping. He suggested that Simon no longer attend if Ahmid came into the office again as he would deal with the man directly as his client. Henry could not believe that Ahmid's activities were illegal in any way, since all that Simon had experienced did not necessarily make Ahmid guilty of drug smuggling. However, in the back of his mind, he wanted to be careful not to be involved in knowingly handling drug proceeds.

Whenever he got the opportunity during the day, Simon called his friends and arranged for them to meet at the "Fish and Fiddle" on that evening. They were all enthusiastic to get together and hear of Simon's experiences. From conversations he had on the phone he got the feeling he was a bit of a hero to them. Inwardly, he felt rather stupid in pursuing an investigation on the slim evidence of a little white powder but it was in his nature to meet challenges head on, so he could not ignore it. When his 'gang' met tonight, he would continue to encourage them to join him in further investigation.

*   *   *   *

When he got home to Francesca, she told him the police had called and said they had been to the warehouse Simon claimed to have broken into and found no evidence of anything illegal going on there. In fact, they said, the place was completely clean and empty.

"Well," exclaimed Simon, "someone must have done a terrific job in cleaning it up because I was feeling something on the floor and noticed signs of stuff growing there."

"Remember, my love," said Francesca, "you were held captive about three days, so they could easily have cleaned the place out. They would have wanted to protect their behinds, in case you'd spoken to anyone before they got hold of you."

"I guess you're right! Anyway, I've called a meeting with the Gang tonight. D'you want to come?"

"Certainly! I'd like to meet them all again!"

"So, let's have supper and go!"

The "Fish and Fiddle" Pub was fairly quiet when they entered and they were able to select a table that would hold six. None of the others had arrived by then, so they ordered a beer and settled back to wait. Five minutes later, Vernon Spreitzer breezed in looking as if he'd come directly from a job. He was wearing a tee-shirt emblazoned with the name of his company and a belt holding innumerable tools hanging round his middle.

Simon stood up and hugged him. "How yer doing smart guy!" he yelled, "come and take a seat! Y'know my dearest Francesca, don't you?"

Vernon sat down and declared, "I sure do know this lovely lady! Didn't I help her when you messed up and got kidnapped?"

"You certainly did, Vernon. You were a great help!" smiled Francesca.

Roy Helwig and Terry Wong arrived together, both looking very clean and tidy. Roy said, "So, how is the hero of the moment?"

"I'm just fine," answered Simon, not bothering to get up to greet them.

"We want to hear all the gory details of your captivity," said Terry, "when we get some beer!"

Gerry Unger's entrance surprised them all because, hanging onto his arm, was an attractive young lady. "Hi, everybody!" he cried out, "Meet my girl friend Val?"

Everyone hustled to move chairs and add more to the table to allow room for all to be seated. Simon stood up and shook Gerry's friend's hand and he was rewarded by a charming smile. "Welcome to the Gang," he said sincerely, "I'm so glad you and Gerry got together."

"Enough of that blarney!" shouted Vernon, "Let's get the beer and wings and hear Simon's story!"

"No doubt, embellished by a few lies?" added Roy amid shouts and laughter.

When they had all been served and settled into eating, Simon began. "I think you know why I became suspicious of my client and I asked for your help –"

"Yea Yea Yea," shouted Roy. "Get on with it!"

"Anyway, Vernon helped me break into a warehouse and left me there"

"Well, I couldn't take a chance of being involved in burglary 'cos my firm insures me to be honest." Explained Vernon.

"Can I get on?" pleaded Simon, waving his hands palm upwards to the group.

"Go ahead," said Terry. "I'm listening."

"The warehouse was black and I only had a torch which I dropped on the floor among a lot of goop. While I was fishing around, a huge guy shines a light on me to blind me and pulls a gun. He marched me through the building but I saw growing plants as well as boxes."

There were murmurs of "Something going on, for sure."

Simon continued. "I was told to get in an SUV and driven to an old farmhouse sort of place where I was shocked to meet Mister Singh, my client! He treated me decently but the big guy locked me in a cellar. On the third morning, I planned to escape and tricked my gaoler to look at a book I was colouring while I nipped out the door and locked him in. Outside, on the road, I got a ride with a Mennonite fellow to St. Agatha where I thumbed a ride back to Waterloo."

"And was I ever glad to see him!" exclaimed Francesca.

"So you were actually kidnapped for three days?" asked Terry, snatching the last of the wings on the serving plate. "Did you tell the Police?"

"Oh, yeah!" said Simon "They made me complete one of their inevitable forms!"

"Hell!" exclaimed Vernon, "All the wings have gone! Shall we order more?"

"No thanks," said Gerry. "Is that okay with everybody?"

There were general murmurs of agreement so Gerry asked, "So Simon. Do you know if they've arrested anybody?"

"Not as far as I know but they did inspect the warehouse and found it completely empty."

"Would you guys be prepared to take a drive up to St. Agatha and try to find what this fellow Singh is doing?" asked Roy out of the blue.

They all sat back in silence as the idea shocked them until Gerry said, "We'd be too much of a crowd if we all went. Maybe take just one car?"

"Gerry, you're a prince! We don't have to break in. Just nose around!" declared Simon.

"I'll go with you." said Francesca. "I know the way as I've worked at Ahmid's house."

"And I'll go with Gerry!" offered Val. "It should be a bit of fun!"

Roy said, "Then I guess you've got enough people. Have Fun!" and he stood up ready to leave. The others said goodbye and drifted out to their cars, leaving Simon, Francesca, Gerry and Val to agree about whose car to take. As soon as this was decided, they left in haste.

Francesca guided them to Ahmid Singh's house. It stood in complete darkness well back from the road. Gerry and Val, who had not been there before, got out of the car and began to wander around. Inside the car, Simon said, "I don't want those two walking up the gravel drive. It will make a noise and may cause Ahmid to come and investigate. Let's get out and join them."

When the four were together Simon whispered, "Keep it quiet! As little noise as possible!"

Gerry asked, "Are we going to try to get into the house?"

Francesca answered, "There's no need. I've not seen anything unusual."

"I'm curious about those two barns back there. Let's all go and do a look around?" Simon suggested. He immediately made his way stealthily through the vegetation towards the barns and the others followed. At one point, they came across a well worn path that seemed to lead from a barn to the house, so they followed it to the first barn. There were no lights so the group explored the exterior as much as they could. Suddenly, Simon gave a hoarse whisper. "Over here! There's an open door!"

They gathered inside and found it stacked with boxes that were labelled with shipping directions. As they explored the labels, they were amazed at how widespread the boxes would be sent. Not only in Canada but to European countries as well.

"Can we find out what's in them?" asked Val.

Simon addressed Fran. "In your work here did you get any idea of what was shipped by Ahmid in theses boxes?"

"Not at all. The records I saw were all code numbers, as far as I could tell."

"Let's go and look in the other barn, "Suggested Gerry.

"Okay. Follow me." Answered Simon.

They moved as quietly as possible across the intervening grassy space between the two barns and soon found an open door in the side. When they were all gathered and had accustomed themselves to the gloom, they could make out a long bench with dishes and pots on it.

The girls examined them, more by touch, than sight, and exclaimed "It's like a cream in these pots!"

"What do you think it is Fran?" whispered Simon.

"Can't tell." She answered. "It's not unpleasant though."

Gerry came to join them from another part of the building. "There's a big grinding and pressing machine over there. They smell spicy or peppery. What the heck`s going on?"

They were suddenly bathed in a strong flashlight beam and a loud rough voice commanded, "Stand still! I've got a gun on you!"

The girls sought protection of their male partners as a huge man appeared before them. Simon exclaimed, "My God! It's my jailer! He works for Ahmid."

"And that's where I'm gonna take you now. Walk out that door and follow the path. Remember, I've got the gun!"

CHAPTER NINETEEN

The four young interlopers followed the path from the barn into Ahmid Singh's kitchen. He was standing there and watching them carefully as they came through the door. As he recognized Simon, he stepped back in surprise and said, "It's you again! You can't seem to stop meddling in my business!"

He turned to Jacob. "Take them into the living room, please Jacob. My wife and I will want to interview them there."

"Are you going to call the police?" Jacob questioned politely.

"Not until I understand what these young people think they are doing." His usually calm voice took on an edge of anger. "I thought I had come to a civilized country where people respected the property of others. Not like parts of India where I could have been burgled every day – or something worse."

Jacob motioned with his gun for the quartet to move through a door which led to the sitting room. Ahmid's wife, Salina, dressed in a long colourful sarong, was sitting in a chair on the far side of the room. She stood up gracefully and approached Francesca.

"Hello, Francesca. I'm very surprised to see you under these circumstances! Come and sit down."

Francesca did just that without explaining her actions in coming to their home at night and Simon followed to sit next to her.

"And you other lady and gentleman! Come and sit down too!" Salina suggested.

Ahmid was saying something to Jacob who left the room, while Ahmid stood in the centre and turned slowly to inspect each of his unwelcome guests.

"I think we should know the names of our intruders," he began. "Simon, of course I do know, not only as my financial advisor but also as my prisoner for three nights!" He smiled at Simon and saw him break a small smile. "And also Francesca who was my employee for a few days." He stared at her for a moment and then added, "She was very helpful, too!"

He stepped across to face Gerry and Val who sat holding hands on a sofa. "Please tell me your names so that we shall be on friendly terms."

Gerry felt reassured by that statement and spoke for the two of them. "I'm Gerry and this is Val. We're friends of Simon."

"I see," Ahmid said deliberately. "I know that friends often do things for one another out of loyalty and I hope that is the only reason for you being here?"

"Well, I did volunteer the idea of driving up to your place because Simon is so anxious to settle his mind about what you do. You are a man of mystery, Mister Singh and our curiosity is peeked!"

Ahmid and his wife laughed in harmony. Salina said, "I would never have said that my husband was mysterious! He has always been meticulously honest and open all the time I've known him."

"Perhaps it is time to explain to our friends what we do." asked Ahmid of his wife. "But before we do that, how about some tea for us all?"

Salina rose from her seat and left the room. Ahmid immediately started talking to them.

"I want you to know that Salina is a fully trained Pharmacist. Not only that but for several years in India she was working at an experimental institution researching the use of natural plants to treat common illnesses. Before we left our homeland she had patented her own ointment which relieved pain."

Salina returned carrying a large brass tray which held a teapot and six mugs. She carefully set this down on a side table and began to pour tea. "I expect some of you take milk and sugar in your tea. I've forgotten to bring it in with me!" Returning with these items she offered a mug to everyone and they added what they wanted.

Simon was amazed at the very civilized way his hosts were treating them and wondered what to expect from them eventually. He whispered to Francesca "You okay?" before sipping the hot tea. She smiled and nodded.

Gerry appeared to be taking everything in his stride. He sat with a confident stance and a keen interest in his eyes. So far he had remained hand in hand with Val, putting down his mug after a quick sip to take Val's hand again.

After a short silence, Ahmid began to speak again. "My wife and I are truly amazed that you four young people have invaded our privacy but we are not angry and have no desire to punish you because you have done us no harm. However, I would like to explain a few things to you all so that you have a better understanding of us and we will leave it to your own consciences to render an adjustment if you feel you should amend your ways." He smiled and checked every face for a reaction. His audience was attentive. "As I explained earlier, my wife owns a patent on a few pain relieving ointments. All the ingredients are from natural products. She uses no chemicals but some of the plants are hard to grow in this country. We tried to raise them in that warehouse you visited, Simon, but it was not a success and we cleared it out." He leaned back in his chair and adjusted his seating.

"The main item in Salina's ointment is capsaicin which is obtained from a certain variety of pepper plant. They grow best in a warmer climate, so we have decided to move to a part of the U.S.A. where these plants can be grown in large quantities to supply my wife's needs." His audience sat up abruptly and looked surprised.

"Couldn't you remain in Canada and import the plants?" asked Simon.

"We could but all that wealth you know I have accumulated I'm going to invest in an integrated farm and production facility so I want to be on the spot!"

"I do understand your objectives," agreed Simon, "but I'd like to know why some of your imported wooden items had a white powder inside them?"

Ahmid laughed. "That was a very unfortunate thing and it was all my brother's fault. You see, we also need a small quantity of morphine that my brother gets from the poppies he cultivates. He thought it would be more cost effective to include some packets of the morphine powder in the wooden box order but he didn't pack the stuff in a strong enough plastic so the packets got torn when they were taken out on arrival here. He was foolish and we have never done that again."

He turned to face Simon. "Is that the reason you came to suspect me of importing drugs?"

"What you've just said, does explain what happened," answered Simon, " but you must admit that you were importing some drugs…" He hesitated, not knowing what else to say and then added, "but did you really have to imprison me?"

"I must apologize to you for having to do that but I wanted to be sure we had cleared the warehouse before you spread a rumour or involved the police."

"Well, I guess that makes us even!"

The room was silent for a minute until Gerry asked, "So what do you intend to do with us now?"

"Firstly, I want you all to give me your assurance that you will not pursue any more ideas of investigating our lives. It is imperative to keep the knowledge I have entrusted to you to yourselves. We cannot have others trying to copy my wife's ointments."

"But, if she has patented them, she's protected, isn't she?" asked Simon.

"How can we be sure? The whole business of patents is riddled with loopholes. The less others know, the more secure we shall feel when expanding our facilities in America."

Simon nodded and looked questioningly at his friends. Gerry shrugged his shoulders as if to say he was satisfied and both girls murmured something under their breaths. I guess I can give you an assurance, on behalf of myself and my friends, that we shall not investigate you again."

"Thank you." said Ahmid, beginning to stand up. "In that case, if you have all finished your tea, we will wish you good night!"

The four visitors also stood and there began a round of friendly hand shakes with their hosts before Salina gracefully showed them to the door.

Driving on the way home, Francesca suddenly put a hand to her mouth. "Simon!" she exclaimed, "what shall we do about the report you gave to the police?"

"Forget it!" he declared. "There's nothing for them to find, so I expect they'll drop it."

"You'd better be right, or else the Singh's will think we've reported them."

"In that case, my love, the best thing I can do is to go to the police station in the morning and clear things up!"

CHAPTER TWENTY

After dropping off Gerry and Val at their respective homes, Simon and Francesca wearily got themselves into bed. Although it was well after one in the morning, neither of them was able to get to sleep. Simon got up and said, "Fran! I've got to sort out this mess I've made with the police, my parents and sister, and my boss! If only I hadn't been so impatient and restless! Now I'll have to go around like a dog with its tail between its legs to explain my actions."

Francesca sat up in bed and answered, "Don't beat yourself over the head, my love! People will soon forget what you've done and they'll accept you for your usual charming self!"

"I sure hope so, Fran! At least I know that you'll stand beside me, whatever comes."

"Huh! I don't know about 'whatever' but, apart from murder, I'll be with you!"

Simon suddenly felt moved to embrace Fran. Crossing to where she sat in bed and, sitting beside her, he put his arms around her shoulders to draw her closer and gently kiss her. After a moment he leaned away a little to gaze into her clear blue eyes and whispered. "You're so beautiful and so caring. Will you marry me?"

Fran immediately put her hands to his cheeks and sighed, "At last, you've said the right thing! Of course I'll marry you!"

They embraced again and kissed until she was almost breathless. Pushing back from him she smiled and asked, "So when will we do it?"

"Get married, you mean?" Simon laughed. "That is what you mean by 'do it'!"

"Oh you beast! What a tease you are! Come back to bed and we'll 'do it' first and decide on a wedding date in the morning!"

The heaving surface of the bed covers was ample indication of their vigorous love making.

The morning proved to be a picture-perfect summer day. The sun was not yet too high in the sky, so there was warmth but no uncomfortable heat. In the garden birds were flitting about pecking in grass and soil to find a breakfast. There was a slight aroma of moist earth and a suggestion of rose perfume. It made Simon feel he was on top of the world and his concerns were unfounded. He made some coffee and took a cup to Francesca who was still drowsing in bed.

"Wake up, dream girl! I'm setting an example of what you can expect when I'm your husband!"

She wriggled herself to a sitting position and took the mug from Simon. "Do you really mean what you've just said?"

"Well – I'll do my best to keep up the service! Now and again, I'll let you get up first so you'll appreciate just what a good husband I am!"

Francesca nearly spilled the coffee when she laughed at his remark. "You'll have to be very patient to wait for me to get up first!"

"Never mind, dear! When shall we get wed?"

"Just as soon as you can get the licence!"

"Bloody hell! Not another form?"

"Much as you hate them, you'll never escape." She finished her coffee. "I find it very hard to understand your obsession against forms."

Simon took a few steps around the bedroom before sitting down on the bed. "I've never told anyone else this but it all goes back to the day I arrived in England."

Francesca turned her head to face him. "Whatever happened?"

"I had to go through customs and immigration and I was quite nervous because I had no idea what to expect. I was edgy, too, because I'd booked my accommodation on the internet and the check-in time was for 2 p.m." Simon stood up again and paced the room. "Instead of going straight through and being able to catch a bus to take me to my digs, I was taken to an office and detained. The two officials told me to show evidence that I was financially sound enough to keep myself for a year. So I produced the letter I had from London School of Economics which stated that I had been awarded a scholarship for my tuition but they wanted to know how I would keep myself in food and accommodation. Well, I didn't know what to say. When I left Canada, Dad gave me a few hundred pounds to get me started and said 'let me know when you need more' and I told the officers this but they were not satisfied."

"So what did they want?" interrupted Francesca.

"As you might expect, they produced a form which was to be signed by a guarantor for my support and said I must get it signed by Dad before I could be admitted into the country. I didn't know what to do and could imagine all my dreams of this special educational opportunity going down the drain."

"Poor, Simon! What a situation to be in."

"Yes, then there was a lot of discussion and questioning about what kind of job Dad had and, when I told them he was a doctor, they asked whether he had a fax machine. I told them he did, so they gave me this wretched form to complete and fax it to him. I completed what information I was sure of and they took his fax number and sent it off. Then they said I could not be released until it was faxed back to them properly signed. Well, I was so nervous imagining what Dad would do and getting more hungry and thirsty by the minute. Finally we got an answer about 5 p.m. and I shot off to my digs knowing I was well past check-in time."

"So what happened when you got there?"

"The proprietor lectured me about not booking in earlier as he could have rented the rooms to someone else but, because I was from Canada, he accepted my booking."

Simon sat down again and Francesca said, "You must have been exhausted but relieved that everything turned out okay. No wonder you hate forms! They can bring a lot of trouble!"

Simon laughed and shrugged and said, "Anyway, are you okay to marry in a Registry Office?"

"Yes," replied Francesca. "I can't abide the thought of all the planning and argument that goes into a formal affair, but I don't know what your parents would say?"

"I guess we should go around and break the news to them. What about if we see them on Saturday? Pop and Sis will be home from work, with any luck, we'll hit the lot of them in one meeting!"

"That's fine, dear. I'm glad I'm free of any such connections!"

"Well, that could be a good reason for a registry office affair because a formal wedding would become very unbalanced when deciding who to invite."

Francesca became pensive. "It's moments like this that I feel sad, having no one else to turn to and to share my happiness. I hope your family will understand."

"I'm sure they will." Simon assured her. "Especially Mother. She's got a big soft heart!"

"Yes, the only time I've met her she was so kind and understanding."

"Well, my love! Let me go and phone while you get up."

When Francesca entered the kitchen after showering, Simon was sitting with another mug of coffee and he immediately reported that his family were all available on Saturday morning and they were invited to go round about ten o'clock.

"Good! So I wont have to get up too early!" she remarked with a wicked smile on her face.

Simon chuckled. "Any excuse to stay in bed, eh?" He stood up. "I'm going round to the police station to clear their records, if I can."

"Okay, love. See you later!"

Upon entering the office, he was accosted by a young policeman whose uniform seemed so new it could not have been worn before that day. "Can I help you, sir?" he asked.

"Yes," began Simon, "not long ago I reported that I'd been kidnapped and, as I'm back now, I didn't want any of your people out looking for me!"

The young policeman smiled and asked, "Do you know the name of the person that took your report?"

"No, actually! He was a heavy sergeant who took me into an office over there." Simon pointed to a doorway off the reception area.

"Oh, I think I know who that would be! What is your name, sir?"

Simon smiled at the thought of being called 'sir' by someone who looked younger than himself. "My name is Simon Lightward." he finally answered.

"Follow me to the office and you can wait there until I can find the Sergeant who has your report." He led Simon to the door he'd pointed to and left him inside the room.

After about ten minutes the heavily-built Sergeant entered with the young policeman trailing him. He took a seat by the table and turned around to shout, "You can sit in on this, Smithers. You may learn something." Then he turned to Simon and said, "So, how did you escape captivity?"

"Well, I tricked the man guarding me and ran for it!"

"Only one guard?"

"Yes. The owner of the whole business didn't come back to check on me."

The Sergeant ruffled through the file he'd brought. "We went to the disused farm building you told us about and found it quite empty. Just as earlier we'd checked on the warehouse and found nothing." He gazed steadily at Simon and added, "Are you sure you're not having us on?"

"Oh no, officer. It really happened the way I reported to you. I think the man behind all this is getting ready to jump ship, as it were."

"And you know who this man is?"

Simon answered slowly, not wanting to reveal any more about Ahmid Singh than he had to. "You see, my suspicions about what he was doing turned out to be quite wrong and he was innocent, so I wouldn't want him harassed by the police. He explained everything to me and treated me very decently. I feel a certain loyalty to him now."

The Sergeant spoke very gruffly. "The police do not 'harass' people! And you have a responsibility as a member of the public to assist the police in any way you can."

"Of course, sir. I know that but can't we just tear up the form I reported my kidnapping on and forget the whole thing?"

"Oh, I don't think so!! These report forms are all numbered and are referenced to crimes through the computer. If I was to tear up your report it could create havoc in our systems here."

"Then, how can I bring closure to my kidnapping?" asked Simon.

"I'll get you Form 1289-S so you can report your release and that will close our investigation." The Sergeant stood up and told the policeman to wait while he was absent. He returned in a matter of moments waving another buff form which he laid in front of Simon. "Here you are, sir. Complete that and you'll be free to go."

Simon studied the Form and realized it was designed for a third party to complete rather than the original complainant. He decided not to raise any questions but to answer as if he was being rescued by a third party. In his mind he imagined how Gerry and the girls might have felt if they had found him locked up at the barns at Ahmid's house. So he modified the story of his discovery and release by explaining that he was found unconscious and tied up after being taken to the house. Gerry and Val must have followed and, when Ahmid and his wife left the room, his friends released him and they all escaped.

He paused for a moment and the Sergeant read what Simon had written. "So, you don't think these two people who took you into their house had anything to do with your kidnapping?" he asked.

"Oh, no, Sergeant. I've no reason to think that!" Simon lied convincingly.

"Alright, then." The sergeant walked out the door. "Thank you for your help. We'll follow up on any loose ends later."

Simon stood up and said to the young policeman, "I guess I'm free to go!" and quickly left the building.

CHAPTER TWENTYONE

It was Saturday morning and Simon and Francesca, dressed in modern summer attire, drove over to his parents' house. There was already a smart little two-seater sports car in the driveway and they speculated on whose it was. Simon parked alongside it and they got out and walked towards the rear of the house. Turning into the back yard they were met by a boisterous cheer from his parents and sister. She took the hand of a smart young man and approached the visitors.

"You've met my fiancé previously, Simon. We got engaged last night. He's Sandy McNeil and another doctor!"

Simon stepped forward and noticed Sandy's typically Scottish red hair as he shook his hand. "So, you're the owner of the sports coupe, eh? Congratulations on your engagement. I hope you'll be as happy as we two 'non-engaged' couple are!"

Francesca piped up and announced, "How can you say that, Simon? We're here to tell everyone we're getting married! So we must be engaged!"

Missus Lightward jumped out of her chair and gave Simon and Francesca a hug. "I'm so pleased!" She said. "Do tell us all about it!"

Samantha grumbled. "Are you stealing the march on me, Simon?"

"Not intentionally," he replied, trying to suppress any reaction to Samantha's jealous comment. "Please tell us of all your plans."

"Just a minute," Mister Lightward intervened. "Let's all sit down and have Mother bring us coffee, then we can exchange all this good news in a tidy fashion!"

With a little juggling of chairs and loungers everyone found seats and waited for the coffee to be brought out by Mother. Simon sat on the edge of the lounger that Francesca had appropriated for herself, while Sandy chose an upright chair and pulled Samantha onto his lap. Father re-arranged the tables so that everybody had a place to set down their mug but his efforts were wasted because Mother wheeled everything out on a trolley and, as she handed each person a mug and a plate of snacks, they were forced to put something on the paving since the tables were too small. However, people settled down to try their drinks, adjust them with more sugar or cream, and finally juggle all they needed into a manageable position.

"Who's going to speak first?" asked Mister Lightward.

"I'm dying to say what we're doing!" exclaimed Francesca, "But I'd like to hear about Samantha's engagement. When did it happen?"

"Only last night!" Samantha burst out. "You could have knocked me down with a feather, when Sandy proposed that we get married!"

"Oh, come on, Sam!" pleaded Sandy. "It wasn't that much of a surprise!"

"Well, maybe you'd been hinting but last night you not only proposed but suggested a wedding date!"

"When is it to be?" asked Simon. "Maybe we could make it a double wedding?"

"Had you got a date in mind?" asked Mother.

"Not really, Mum. We don't want a formal wedding, so we could set any day that meets everyone's needs."

"I said we don't have to have a formal wedding, either," Sandy butted in and received a frown from Samantha.

"Wait a bit," yelled Father. "Don't you ladies want all the trimmings and excitement of a formal wedding?" He looked around expectantly. "What about you, Mother?"

Missus Lightward laughed. "Considering the economical affair we had, I can't say that it matters to me what the girls want."

Sandy took Samantha's hands in his and peered into her eyes. "You've always said you didn't want any fuss when we got married. What about us teeming up with Simon and Francesca and making it a double affair?"

Samantha gazed at Sandy for a minute and smiled. "Okay. I'm game to do that!"

"Wow!" yelled Simon. "It looks like we only have to fix a date!"

"That may not be as easy as it sounds!" said Samantha. "With our shifts at the Hospital to work around and getting your parents to come from Scotland, and whatever Simon and Francesca have to fit in."

"Och! Don't worry aboot my folk! They long ago stopped being concerned aboot me!"

"How about you and Samantha settle on a date suitable to your shifts and tell us what it is. I don't think Fran and I have many problems with timing." Suggested Simon.

"Okay! We'll get back to you!"

"So it seems we'll have a double wedding to attend, Mother!" declared Father.

"I think it's all going to seem very exciting! I'll need some new clothes!"

Samantha laughed. "You'll not be the only one! The ladies dress shops around here will be in great demand!"

Simon walked over to Sandy and asked, "Have you got a license yet?"

"Och, no! Where do we go for one of those?"

"I'm not sure but I guess I'd start at City Hall. D'you want to come with me?"

"Won't we have to wait till Monday?" asked Sandy. "These officials never work at weekends!"

"I guess you're right! So I'm not sure when to apply."

"Well, I'll leave it to you, Simon. Give me a buzz when you're gong to get your licence and I'll make time to go with you."

"I'm glad that's all we have to take care of! Not like all these girls'dresses!" He left Sandy to rejoin Francesca. "Come along, love. Let's go home and sort ourselves out?"

"Have you any idea when we could fix a date for the wedding?" Francesca asked when they arrived back at her place.

"Not really! I need to ask questions at City Hall on Monday before I can get an inkling about advanced notice or anything else that we might come up against."

"Yes, I see that. Are you really happy about the idea of a double wedding?"

"Why not? I thought it might be fun!"

"Had you thought about any honeymoon?" asked Francesca seriously.

"Gosh! No!" said Simon, standing closer to her and gripping her arms. "Am I being terribly neglectful?"

Francesca put her arms around him. "No, darling, it's not important. Just knowing I'll be yours for life is all I ask!"

"At least, let's go away for a night of luxury in one of those Niagara hotels that cater to honeymooners?"

"That's a lovely idea! Let's do it!"

"Okay. As soon as we have a date I'll make a booking."

Two weeks passed before Simon was able to get a date for their marriage, along with Sandy and Samantha and time seemed to drag. Both girls had meetings to discuss and explore the kinds of dresses they would buy but Samantha did not want a honeymoon night following their wedding. Apparently, she and Sandy had bigger ideas of taking a month away in Europe which was easier to arrange within their work schedules. Finally, all details were cleared and the actual day was upon them.

The wedding office in the city hall was pleasantly decorated to create a bright and festive atmosphere, far removed from any plain office décor. There was only one small desk discretely tucked away in one corner and screened by an artificial fiscus tree, together with several sofas and arm chairs for people to sit and relax. It was recognized, by officials, that for many, the act of getting married could be both exciting and nerve-wracking.

When Simon and Francesca walked in, his parents were already there and relaxing in separate arm chairs. Missus Lightward was in a pale blue two piece suit of a light fabric and she wore a red rose on one shoulder. Her husband was not much different from his every-day doctor's suit but he did sport a very pink shirt under his jacket. They both got up to greet their son and soon to be daughter –in –law and remained on their feet when their daughter came in with Sandy. Simon thought he had never seen Samantha looking so fresh and pretty, so he went to her and gave a kiss and a hug.

"You look wonderful, Samantha. The prospect of marriage must be giving you a lift!"

"Thank you, Simon. It's so nice that we have found compatibility after all these years."

Sandy joined them and said, "Isn't she radiant, Simon?"

Simon shook his hand. "You're a lucky fellow and I wish you every happiness."

The official came into the room and asked the two couples if they had their marriage certificates. Sandy immediately pulled a form from his inside jacket pocket and handed it over. Simon remained fishing in every pocket of his suit with a great degree of concern but was unable to produce the appropriate document.

"What's the matter?" asked Francesca.

"I can't seem to find the damned form!"

"You sure you put it in your pocket before we came out?"

"I thought so!" He began another check of his pockets.

When it was clear that he could not produce the licence, the official said, "I'm afraid we only have limited time, so I must carry on with the marriage of Sandy and Samantha. Perhaps you need to go home and find your licence?"

Simon felt a complete idiot. He wished he could immediately vaporize and remove himself from the room but he turned to the other pair and mumbled an apology before grabbing Francesca's hand and almost running from the room. Once outside he stopped and put his arms round her and said, "You must think me a stupid fool not to make sure I had the licence. Now I've ruined your day!"

"No you haven't. I'm not concerned about being married at the same time as Sandy and Sam. We can get married any time!"

"But what about the reservation I've made for tonight?"

"We can still use it can't we? We've slept together unmarried for some months now, what's another night?"

"Do you want me to go back and find that damned form?" asked Simon seriously.

"Of course not, silly! Let's get in our car and drive to Niagara!"

"So it won't be a matter of form after all?"